St. Stephen's

Also by the author
Digressions of a Naked Party Girl
Guilty

Plays
Playmurder
The Dressing Gown

Lynn
How wonderful
to have ideal
reader!
_xo_
Sky

St. Stephen's

Sky Gilbert

a mis Fit
b o o k

INSOMNIAC PRESS

Edited by Michael Holmes
Copy edited by Peter Darbyshire
Designed by Schrödinger's Cat

Canadian Cataloguing in Publication Data

Gilbert, Sky,
     St. Stephen's

ISBN 1-895837-70-7

I. Title.

PS8563.I4743S24 1999   C813'.54   C99-931681-8
PR9199.3.G54S24 1999

The publisher gratefully acknowledges the support of the Canada Council and the Ontario Arts Council.

THE CANADA COUNCIL | LE CONSEIL DES ARTS
FOR THE ARTS | DU CANADA
SINCE 1957 | DEPUIS 1957

Printed and bound in Canada

Insomniac Press, 393 Shaw Street,
Toronto, Ontario, Canada, M6J 2X4
www.insomniacpress.com

ONTARIO ARTS
COUNCIL

CONSEIL DES ARTS
DE L'ONTARIO

For Ian Jarvis

"Let him kiss me with his mouth."

— St. Bernard

Part One

I don't think I'll ever learn. I mean, I'll never learn what learning is supposed to teach you.

What's the smartest thing anyone ever taught me? The thing that I look back on now and say, wow, that was really intelligent? Well, it was when I was an usher at The Shea's Theatre. I was at university (supposedly learning all sorts of things). And to support myself I worked as an usher at the movies, like a lot of other young guys. (A lot of other young guys who were gay, by the way. It seems to me now that most of those ushers were gay. I have a photo of me taken at the time. I thought I was straight. Looking like a penguin in my little Charlie Chaplin suit, smiling with lots of curly hair. I had a lot to learn.) Anyway, Mr. Lowenstien was the manager of The Shea's, and he was always walking around, looking busy, with keys in his hands. I never quite figured out what he did, but it seemed to have a lot to do with telling the candy-girls to smile and talking about "show business." He always prefaced everything by reminding us that he was in "show business." Which I always thought was pitiful. I mean, he was just a short, fat, bald guy in a bad suit, running around harassing the candy-girls and jingling his keys. But he thought he was another Cecil B. deMille. He did give me some good advice (which I didn't know was good at the time).

One night, a bunch of us ushers were standing around gabbing away (probably flirting with each other, even though we didn't know that's what we were doing). And for some reason, Mr. Lowenstien thought we were flirting with the candy-girls. (It was wishful thinking on his part. I'm sure the guy had an inkling he was a nobody. But to have a totally gay staff would have been really depressing for him.) So he told us this joke. He said it was an old joke. Now, when an old guy tells you an old joke, you know you're in for a snoozer. And you have to act like it's so funny; in this case, because sad old Mr. Lowenstien is your goddamn key-jingling employer.

So Lowenstien saunters up, wearing his "I'm going to relate to you cool young guys as a person, not just as a pitiful old employer" face, and he says, "Let me tell you boys a joke!" And, of course, we all perk up, thinking, yeah, something silly to distract us from sweeping popcorn off the floor and pretending to flirt with the candy-girls, oh boy. "This is the joke," says Mr. Lowenstien. "There's this young bull and an old bull, and they're standing at the top of the hill looking at some young cows." (Of course the joke has to be sexist, that's part of the deal.) "And the young bull says to the old bull, 'I'm going to run down there and get me a cow.'" (That's what Mr. Lowenstien said— "Get me a cow.") "And the old bull looked at the young bull and said, 'I'm going to *walk* down there and get me *all* of 'em!'" And then Mr. Lowenstien laughed. He laughed so fucking hard

I thought he was going to bust his britches. And all the pre-tending-to-be-straight ushers laughed, because we wanted to seem like we were good old boys, and we wanted to keep our jobs. And then Mr. Lowenstien jingled away. Nobody really talked about the joke afterwards; it was kinda like *The Emperor's New Clothes*. But I sure as hell didn't know what that stupid joke meant.

Now that I'm what you'd call an older guy, I know what it means: the slow topman gets the ass. You know, there's no seduction like the old slow seduction.

This is exactly how learning works. It's weird. Someone can tell you something thousands of years ago and you don't get it. Then suddenly, years later (maybe when you're fucking some-one really slow, for instance), a light bulb pops: "Oh, *that's* what that stupid joke was about."

I had this teacher at university. He was one of my best fucking teachers—a real old fart, but really smart. Anyway, he said that literature was all about reading something, then living again, then going back to the text. In other words, you have to slip some living in between those books and compare what books say about life to what life actually is. I think that's very good advice. See, Mr. Lowenstien's advice was like a corny old book. And I had to do a little fucking before I came back to that corny old book and really learned something.

Now, I have this fantasy. That somehow, at the exact same moment as I had this revelation about the bulls and the cows, Mr. Lowenstien figured out all his ushers were fags. Or maybe he even became a fag himself. I know that's a strange thing to think. But teaching and learning are the same thing. Exactly. So much the same thing, in fact, that if you haven't learned any-thing, you haven't *taught* anything. In my opinion. What I'm saying is, if you're a teacher and it's the end of the year, and you give the fucking students a test to see if they've learned anything from you, part of that test should be: have you learned anything from them?

And that's a very important concept—the point of this whole goddamn book.

Teaching is learning; learning is teaching.

And if you think a book is just a fucking phrase or paragraph or whatever, you should stop right now.

T his brings me to St. Stephen's. Why? Well, basically because it took me a long time to get to St. Stephen's. And once I was there I had to leave for a while. And then come back again. And when I was back, I went through some pretty rough shit before I figured things out. So, it took me a long time, but I learned something. Which means, I guess, I taught something. Though I think most people at St. Stephen's would deny it. They'd probably say I was a total fuck-up. Most people would probably say I learned nothing; that I, in fact, corrupted some people. Or maybe just one person. I don't know.

I guess I should tell you about St. Stephen's. The first thing to know is that it's not a real place. And by that I don't mean it's a fairy place or something. This is not a *fairy* tale—in that sense of the word. No, it isn't that St. Stephen's is some sort of fairyland—in any sense of the word. (All the goddamn teachers except for me were *supposedly* straight!) It's that St. Stephen's is set up in a little town that's a resort for millionaires. And it's a very white place. Very upper-class. Stony Bay. It's so upper-class that people call it Tony Bay. It's very tony.

And St. Stephen's, if you haven't guessed already, is a university. It's small, but it has a very good reputation (or it did, until I got there). You know, it's the type of university that small-town, rich white people send their kids to, so that the kids can stay kids for a little while longer. In fact, I only saw one Black student the whole time I was there. I saw some Asian kids and a few who looked kind of brown. I'm not saying the place was racist, I just mean that people were so white that they would treat anybody, even a Black person, with a huge amount of kindness—just to make up for the mistakes of American history. But that doesn't change the fact that (somehow) there aren't a lot of black people who send their kids to a tony university by a lake in the country.

How did I get to St. Stephen's? Well, it's a long story. You see, I used to be an actor. I was an okay actor, but the whole acting thing really wasn't for me.

I don't know if you're aware of this, but most actors are horrible people. They would sell their soul to get to Hollywood. And what's Hollywood but a bunch of hookers and facelifts?

Oh yeah, money. How could I forget about money?

But you'll find, if you've worked as an actor in the theatre, that most actors will screw anybody, suck up to anybody, and basically sell their soul to get to the top. Most actors don't want to be in "the theatre." They just hope that if they do plays they'll get discovered. Most don't. I did, though, in a sense, get discovered by the head honcho of St. Stephen's. So anyway, I did some acting for a while, and then I realized I was wasting my intelligence. Honestly.

My departure from show biz is actually kind of interesting. I was doing this gay farce at a Jewish theatre that was also partly a cultural centre. The artistic director of the theatre had decided to challenge the clientele (which was mostly elderly and Jewish) by putting on a hot gay New York farce. This play *did* have a Jewish mother in it—you know, a classic cranky Jewish mother. But that wasn't enough to please the crowd. You see, I played an overweight gay man (I'm not overweight— hey had to put me in a fatsuit) who chased this other beautiful fag

around a bed for the whole second act. Well, the audience was
fine with the first act. It had a Jewish mother in it to keep them
happy. Then came *my* act and they were in hell. You could tell.
The play suddenly became their worst nightmare. You could
see that they were really scared I might catch the pretty boy I
was chasing. My character never did, though. One matinee there
were fourteen walkouts. The audience was mainly cranky old
Jewish ladies and their practically dead husbands. I mean, the
hatred coming from the audience was palpable. And my scene
was supposed to be funny. Oh, after the matinees there were
these talkback sessions (I hate those things) where the audience asks you questions. Now, inevitably, the audience would
ask me stupid questions like, "You really get around the stage
fast for a big guy. How do you do it?" And then I'd have to
explain to them that I was wearing a fatsuit. It was so insulting.
Okay, I admit my face *is* fat (whereas my body is big, but not
fat). But they all thought I really weighed four hundred pounds.
(I actually weigh in at about 240, but still…) And it became
clear that the old broads had been too nervous to laugh *during*
the show because they thought they were actually laughing at a
fat person. You know, making fun.

Now, these questions were irritating, but not quite infuriating.
But then they started asking questions like, "Do you find it
difficult to play a gay character?" And I'd say, "Not really, since
I happen to be a fag," which made a couple of the old ladies
practically lose their teeth and nudge their husbands so hard
that the old geezers actually woke up. Well, we did this one
matinee where some really uptight old lady asked me, "Do you
think these characters are good role models for our young
people?" I was completely flabbergasted. These were characters in a farce, for fucksakes! They weren't supposed to be role
models. They were supposed to show you how fucked up the
world is. I mean, how smart do you have to be to get that?

The lead actress in the play was my best friend at the time. Her name is Gillian, or Jilly. She's fucking brilliant. She asked me, "Haven't they ever seen a play before?" And I reminded her that most of the audience spent most of their time watching television. Then she asked, "But don't they see different types of characters on television? Don't they at least get exposed to comedy and fiction?" So I explained to Jilly that most old people (like my relatives back home in the Midwest, for instance) may watch TV, but they make sure not to tune into anything offensive. I have an aunt who only watches *Murder She Wrote*, and *Diagnosis Murder*. And everybody knows these are not *real* murder shows. (No blood and swearing, just folksy small-town detective types with cute quirks and funny pets.) I tried to make Jilly understand that it's possible to watch quite a lot of TV and still know nothing about life or art.

Now all of this had nothing to do with the audience being Jewish. Or old, for that matter. It had to do with them being middle-class. But the reason I decided to quit acting did have to do with them being Jewish (or with Jewish culture, sort of). You see, one day when I was out there doing an audience talkback session this one old bat starts to go on about how she finds the play disgusting. About how she finds my gay character disgusting. It makes her sick and all that. So of course I was burning mad. And I admit I sort of lost it. I said, "Have you noticed, by the way, that there is a Holocaust Memorial outside this building?" Well, of course they had noticed. The theatre was in a Jewish cultural centre. They spent half their time out at the Holocaust memorial, remembering. Which is great, right?

But try remembering *everything*.

So I said, "Are you aware that Hitler didn't just send Jews to the ovens, that he sent homosexuals as well? Those homosexual people you also think are disgusting? Could you try thinking about that concept for a minute? Or maybe that's too much trouble?"

Well, you could have heard a pin drop. I guess those old Jewish people weren't too fond of being reminded that their comrades in the gas chambers were a bunch of faggots.

And no, I didn't get invited back to perform at that theatre again.

Since acting was no longer a positive life choice, I decided to leave the profession for a while. So I got a job with one of those little unaccredited co-operative workshop thingys. You know what I mean. Every city has one. It was called The Learning Co-op and it was started by this wingy lady named Mona Beyer. She was a trip. All frizzy hair and "I'm just going crazy today, I'm going nuts." I met with her at some little café and stated my situation. "I can't stand acting anymore, because I'm too political, so I'd like to start a course for actors who think about politics. For actors thinking about starting their own companies. Actors into political action." Actually, I didn't care about any of this shit, but I sure needed to make some money. Well, Mona bought it. The big thing about working with Mona was that you had to have tea with her now and then and listen to all her problems. That was a part of your job as a teacher at "The Co-op." Well, my workshops went okay. In fact, they went more than okay. People seemed to really like them. I developed a "following," became a bit of a "guru." Don't ask me to explain why. I certainly didn't try to be. I mean, I hate gurus. But my classes were all about how stupid and pretentious the acting profession could be, and I guess a lot of people thought I was a breath of fresh air. Anyway, it was at one of these little classes that I met Matthew Harding.

When I say the name I kind of get shivers. (No, I'll be honest, I really do.) He was the premier mentor of my life, the real thing. And I say that because I loved him—not just intellectually, but emotionally. And yes, physically. And, of course, today I have mixed feelings about him and I distrust a lot of things about him. But at the time he taught me a lot. About art, and about me.

The concept of a mentor is not something you just kick around. I mean, when I started these little political acting classes, "fans" came up to me and told me that I was their "mentor." And I tried not to yell at them, "Hey, do you love me? I mean do you really love me? Have you licked my tits? Have you got drunk with me? No? Okay, then don't give me that shit about me being your mentor, because I'm not."

I hope that doesn't make me seem like a misanthropic fuck-up. (I suppose I am in a way.) But what I'm trying to say is that calling someone a mentor is a big thing. It means a lot more than just coming to some guy's political acting classes and liking them. It means actually loving them.

I loved Matthew, I really did. But I'm getting ahead of myself.

So there I was, doing this class in "Political ACTion" in a church basement somewhere. Most churches wouldn't have had me, but the place was Unitarian. Don't get me started about Unitarians. I think they're more of a radical social club than a church, but it's nice that crazy old lefties can have a place to commune with God. It's just so hard to imagine a church without *any* moral code to make you feel guilty. Anyway, the crazy Unitarians let me do my radical classes in their basement and as I said, I developed this kind of extreme fan club. It was small but loyal. A tiny coterie of people would take my classes over and over. But the important thing to understand is that there were always twenty people there in the church basement, so it seemed packed. It must have looked like a very romantic thing, actually. I mean, I didn't really care about the political action deal. Let's just say I'm the kind of person who's always liked to stir up shit. And I'm sure I appeared very radical and slightly heroic because I can get very passionate about politics and stuff (especially the dispossessed—you know, queers and minorities) at the drop of a hat.

Well, I didn't notice Matthew in the crowd because I just
didn't know him at the time. But he was there.

He was one of the auditors. For the first class, Mona would
always let one or two people audit. They had to pay a small
fee, of course. (Mona was making quite a good living off this
little school, actually.) So sometimes there would be one or
two people at the first class who weren't actually registered
but wanted to audit. And the class went well. Then everyone
left except for this tall man—very handsome. He looked about
forty-five, with light brown hair. And he had a sort of greasy-
looking, but kind of cute, Italian guy with him. So at the end
of the evening, no one was there but us three.

This handsome guy crossed the room, and then he sort of
burst out with praise. Or he *seemed* to burst out with it. I look
back on it now, and I wonder how sincere it all was since he
never really mentioned the whole "political ACTion" aspect
of my little course ever again. Never in our whole relationship did Matthew talk to me about my radical politics.

But that night he let loose. And when he wanted to be excited
about something it was really a sight for sore eyes. Matthew
was classically handsome, and lean. He looked like Paul
Newman. And he had this fabulous British accent, and this
voice, because he used to be an actor.

"That was fabulous. That was absolutely fabulous. You really were wonderful. There's something terribly special about
your teaching and I'm having trouble defining it." He turned
to his friend and asked, "Frank, do you know, do you have any
idea what it is?" Frank looked kind of stumped and goofy,
but he cleared his throat, as if he was used to being put in
positions like this.

"It was fabulous. Both serious and funny."

"Yes, serious and funny. Your teaching switched tone as
quickly as it switched ideas. But I don't know if it's that. I don't

know if it's really that. You are saying so much, but the pill is so sugar-coated that one often misses the pill for the coating. But the coating itself, of course, *is* the education."

"Are you saying the medium is the message?" I was half-sarcastic, because his fucking enthusiasm was kind of scary.

"I am saying that, yes, I am. But somehow it's more complicated. It's like music, your teaching is like music. Listen, I must have you—that is, you must come; you must teach, at St. Stephen's."

"What?" I said. I was kinda flabbergasted.

"You must teach in an accredited institution, that's what I'm trying to tell you. It's all fine and good to do your work here in a church basement, but a wider audience should hear. We must have you at St. Stephen's. St. Stephen's is a very special place and we must have you there. You just must be a part of it, but I won't explain now. Frank will give you a card, won't you, Frank—there—and you will call me. Please do call. Will you? I think it's absolutely right and important that you do." And as he said this he kind of stared right into me.

And even though the words did sound overblown and formal and unbelievably complimentary, he had this fucking way of looking at you that was honest and charming. And he was so handsome. He really was perfectly handsome. He could have been a matinee idol, really.

And then he smiled at me, shyly. Shyly, that was the kicker. And then he sort of humbly shuffled out of the room. And I really have to describe that shuffle, because it was pure Matthew.

I mean, here he was, the dean of an incredibly prestigious, rich university—prestigious and rich (and a little bit famous) himself. And incredibly handsome and articulate. And he even had this entourage. (I mean, this Frank fellow was completely an entourage, even though he was only one person. He had a slightly nauseating obsequiousness, which I didn't even notice at the time. But it sure made it seem like Matthew was being followed by a sort of train of people.) Yes, despite all that, he managed to sort of shuffle out of the room, humbly. (He always wore these great preppy clothes, I mean clothes that would have made me look stupid. You have to be lean to wear stuff like that. You know, running shoes, khaki pants, and a lime shirt, or something.) And in that shuffle, he sort of told you, "Hey, ignore me if you want. I may be beautiful and powerful and articulate, but I'm really a nobody like you—and I certainly don't expect you to respond to my humble request."

It was breathtaking.

I was left all alone in that crazy little church (I think it was designed by a Frank Lloyd Wright devotee or something—it was really very charming) with my keys—they let me lock up. And suddenly it seemed like my little life was really pretty drab and uneventful. At least it had been until Matthew showed up.

And of course I took the job.

But I should explain to you something about the circumstances of taking the job at St. Stephen's, because it really was a big thing for me.

You see, I was absolutely ripe for this kind of opportunity. My life had just gone through a big change and I didn't have any money. So, the gist was: I was poor as a church mouse, trying to scrape by teaching this one course because I refused to take another damned acting job. Teaching at a rich school would be fabulous for my bank account.

Never mind my reputation. I had heard of St. Stephen's, and I knew it wasn't Yale, but it *was* prestigious. Instead of being some weird figure who taught in church basements, I had the chance to make a regular salary and become somewhat respectable and secure. Which I had never been. Never.

And then there was Matthew himself. I fell a little in love with the guy the moment I saw him. Of course, I never thought he could be attracted to me. I actually believed Frank was his boyfriend. (This was his little trick; Frank wasn't.) So the whole idea of St. Stephen's was incredibly attractive to me.

I called Frank the next day. Frank was very nice on the phone, but not quite as charming as Matthew. He said that he was the administrator of the school and that he'd meet me for a drink. We decided to go to this gay bar called Rumours, which was sort of the gay Cheers in the city where I lived. That's pretty important, actually. I guess I should make it clear. If I was going to do this St. Stephen's thing, it meant that I was going to have to move to the country. And that was also a big deal. And it made me a little nervous.

The country has always been an issue in my life. I'm a small-town boy. That is, I was born in this little town in the Midwest. It was the kind of place where there was a town "common" and everybody knew everybody's business. Kinda like *Peyton Place*, only not half as much fun. I mean, I have the whole small-town conservative background. My grandmother was a Daughter of the American Revolution and she pinned a poppy on Truman. She did. There's an actual photo of it. She was very big on "good works." Have you ever seen *Music Man*? The mayor's wife—named Eulalie McKechnie Shinn (played by Hermoine Gingold)—was a lot like my grandmother. (Remember how great Hermoine Gingold was in that movie? She tried to get Shirley Jones—Marion the Librarian—to ban Balzac. And the way she said Balzac made it sound just like "ball sac." I just loved her for that. And then she gathered all the town ladies together to do these tableau dances where they would imitate Greek urns. It was too funny. I mean, Hermoine was the perfect small-town culturemonger—totally stupid and pretentious.) Now, I'm not saying my grandmother was that bad. But, like Hermoine Gingold, she wasn't really pretty or anything. In fact, I've looked at pictures of her when she was young and she was kinda homely. But she always managed to pull off her look with manners and style. Her big thing was, like, if she had to say something nice about an ugly baby, she'd say, "What an interesting baby!" She managed to never insult anyone. She used to be the head of this group called Positive Labour, which I thought was some sort of union institution when I was a kid. But nothing could be further from the truth. The reason I say this is because late in life my grandmother used to do volunteer work for a right-wing pamphlet company. She even tried to get me to read some of those pamphlets. I couldn't stomach them because they were basically all about being a *Good American*. My grandmother wasn't very nice to me, actually. I gave her a poem once, for instance. I was very proud of it. It was a sonnet and it had won a prize in school. She just read it and said, "It doesn't have the proper number of syllables in each line to be a sonnet." That's the kind of woman she was.

She and my grandfather lived in this big house on the main thoroughfare. My grandfather was the worst Fascist of all. All his life he worked at least ten jobs, a complete obsessive workaholic. Boy, could he get mad. He was the kind of guy who, when they refused to fly an American flag in his local Baptist church, refused to go to church anymore. When my grandmother died, he decided to donate a flag to the Positive Labourers in her memory. An electric self-erecting flag, if you can believe it. Every night, it folded itself up and put itself to bed in this little electric box. And, in the morning, it would suddenly self-erect and stand up all hard and straight and wave around. This always sounded kinda dirty to me. But to my grandfather and this little Midwestern town, I guess the self-erecting flag was very patriotic.

I go on about this just to give you an idea how oppressive a conservative, small-town upbringing can be. Anyway, it's this that has caused me to have a horror of small towns. To me small-towns mean Fascism, hypocrisy, and self-erecting flags. I knew if I was going to teach at St. Stephen's, I would have to move to little Stony Bay. It was at least an hour and a half from the city where I lived at the time, and the whole idea terrified me.

Okay, I should be honest. It's not *just* because I was brought up in a small town, but also because I'm a slut.

And I might say, "What gay man isn't?"—but I know that's not true. Let's just say I'm one of the sluttier ones. I like sex and I admit it. I like my local bathhouse, my local bar, my local glory hole. I also happen to be a fucking intellectual. (I know that might be hard to believe, but it's true. I'm just very unpretentious.) And I like movies and plays and tuning in to lots of television stations. I couldn't live without A&E. And poetry readings. And dance. (Well, I can take or leave dance.) I like the cultural stuff a big city has, and the sex. A lot of fags are very snooty about not liking the city. I think some fags just love to go on and on about how they love to live in the country just to show how faithful they are to their lovers. But there's always the cruisy little "town common."

I knew this one fag who was moving to some hick town once (to act in a play) and I said, "Girlfriend, how are you going to survive there?" He practically cut my dick off for asking that. "I'm sorry," he sniffed, "but some of us don't need to live next to a bathhouse."

Well, I'm sorry but I do. And it's not just the sexual convenience of having the bathhouse next door; it's not. It's the whole atmosphere—living in a gay neighbourhood and seeing your local gay lonely cases and your local drag queens panhandling on the street. For instance, we have this really funny-looking drag queen in our city named Wendy who sings off-key to a ukelele, and we all love her. And the gay barber shop and the rude gay clerks. I mean, you can't have a gay part of town without snippy little effeminate gay clerks who are too busy to wait on you. I have a theory about this. I think most of the gay guys who work on the gay streets in any big burg are from small towns. And they are just so goddamned happy they don't have to be closeted hairdressers anymore that they get all snippy from the sheer joy of living with their own people. But I even like the bitchy little fag store clerks in big towns. In fact, I love them.

Especially this one little guy we have whose name I don't know, even though I must have met him five hundred times. He's probably about sixty years old and he's very little. He shaves his head and wears work boots, like an 1980s Village People construction worker clone. Whether it's summer or winter, he's got his shirt open, showing his pasty little chest and saggy old tits. His energy is very intense. When I'm feeling very caustic I call him "The Midget With Gay Tourette's" or just "Gay Tourette's" for short. You see, his Tourette's isn't the usual swearing or convulsing kind you get on Sally Jesse Raphael. It's all made up of gay phrases. Like, he'll come up to you and say, "Hello, girlfriend, oh Mary!" Which, of course, requires no response. And sometimes he says, "So, you workin?" Which also requires no response because he always says it to you when you're sitting on a stoop or a bench. And what he means is, "Are you hooking?" So it's kind of a joke. A gay joke in the sense that all fags are hookers. I mean, you'd have to be an "out" gay doctor—you'd need very special knowledge—if you were going to understand and treat his particular form of Tourette's. And he's so nervous and twitchy that if you don't respond to him (most people don't) then he lets go with this string of "gayisms" that don't really make sense. "Hello, tell me about it, hello, I've been there, don't start with me, girl." My theory about him is that he was this cute gay boy once (a long time ago) and he never developed any actual skills except fucking and talking like a fag. (You can read about fags like him in a great book by Edmund White called *States Of Desire*. Edmund talks about these young gay guys who never really learn any marketable skills. All they do is hop from one sugar daddy to the next. It's a very interesting book.) So I figure "Gay Tourette's" is one of those aging pretty boys who is not only lacking a profession and skills but also a brain. I feel very sorry for him because he obviously hasn't a hope in hell of communicating with anyone. Once I was with a particularly brave friend and "Gay Tourette's" started talking about getting a job. He said, "I'm too old, nobody wants me. I tried to get a job at McDonald's but I have attacks." And my friend, who was feeling a little cruel, but also trying to break through this guy's weirdness, said, "Like a Mac attack?" And "Gay Tourette's" just ignored him and kept going on about his lack of job. "No, it was blackouts," he said. "I get blackouts."

I'm actually very afraid of "Gay Tourette's." It's partially because he shaves his pointy head and he looks like Mr. Pinhead, the circus freak. Mr. Pinhead always scared me, ever since childhood. (Yeah, Bozo The Clown used to give me anxiety attacks.) But also it's because I look at him and think, there but for the grace of God go I. (Or any other fag for that matter.) He's sort of the Holy Fool, the Christ of the gay ghetto. He carries all our sins.

So you just have to love him.

I even love the local gay political magazines. We have one gay political mag in our city, and it hates me because I am a loud, sexual, out-of-the-closet homosexual. Every city has one of these gay political papers. It's not a gay glossy—it refuses to be one of those papers with pictures of pretty boys. This paper *claims* to be interested in dealing with political issues and giving equal time to lesbians (except it doesn't). This local gay political magazine is usually not political at all. It's usually just another gossip rag that spends all of its time tearing down the local gay institutions in the name of "objective journalism." I have to say, though, that even though the local gay political rag is always writing about how fat and ugly I am, I love it anyway. I'm not being messianic or anything; I'm not turning the other cheek. I just realize that hating and killing your own is part of developing a gay community.

And I love that idea of community you get in a city with a gay street, a nasty gay paper, and snippy gay clerks.

So all of this was running through my mind when I thought about moving to Stony Bay. I knew people called it Tony Bay. And I knew there wouldn't be a gay street in Tony Bay. Or a bathhouse. I think it was even too small a town to have a "town common." And I didn't know if I would be able to stand it.

The drink with Frank was kinda weird. Partially because he was weird, and partially because the whole thing intimidated me. (And partially because I came on to him.)

We found this little dark corner at Rumour's. I was immediately impressed and intimidated to find that this Frank guy would wear a suit to a gay bar. And to find out that I was attracted to him. He was kinda beefy and just very luscious. But he was all business with me. Not mean or anything, just as nice as was necessary. After all, we were talking about a job. He told me again that Matthew was very impressed with me and very excited to have me at St. Stephen's. I asked him a little bit about the school and he wasn't very specific. He *did* say that the teachers at St. Stephen's were very "special." I asked him— what he meant by special. Did he mean "the cream of the crop"? And he said, "No, I mean they are a very special group of people. For them, teaching is not just a job, it's a mission." He sounded like he was quoting from something. It was scary because I couldn't imagine teaching ever becoming a mission for me.

Which shows how much I had to learn.

Anyway, I could see that any information about St. Stephen's was going to be shrouded in some sort of portentious mystery with Frank. So I decided not to pursue it. He told me that Matthew would clue me in when I got there. So I thought the time was right to tell him that I never finished my M.A. And his response completely impressed me (and scared me a bit). He said, "Don't worry, that doesn't matter, Matthew will take care of that." I asked him how, and he said, "Don't worry." It seemed pretty amazing to me that not only were they going to hire me on the basis of, well, nothing, but they were going to give me some sort of instant M.A. to boot.

Frank said that I should come down soon (it was late October) and sit in on some of Matthew's classes. And then I could start in the winter semester (which was January). I asked about getting a place to stay and they said they'd help me find a little house to stay in. (A little house? I'd never had any kind of house of my own.) And when he told me the salary I just about flipped. Let's just say it was more money than I was ever used to having. After that, I was pretty happy because life seemed so easy. We got kind of drunk. Now, the drunker I got, the more attractive Frank seemed. (He looked like he'd be chunky and furry under his suit. Not my usual type, but certainly fuckable.) And he wouldn't leave. He got so drunk that he told me that he was very ambitious and that someday he wanted to be president. This seemed sort of strange to me, coming from the administrator of a small (if prestigious) university. But I think it was this crazy ambition that gave me a hard-on. I asked him if he would like to come back to my place for a while. He very deftly rejected me, acting like it was a completely ridiculous suggestion. But I didn't find him insulting.

Later, I realized that Frank couldn't possibly have fucked me because Matthew was after me. I was being saved for the big experience with the top gun.

It was a very exciting time, kind of like being in a fairy tale. All of a sudden, I had money and my own house and Stony Bay. Well, it seemed kind of enchanted. It was getting near the end of the fall, but there were still some very orange leaves on the trees. My new house turned out to be a two-bedroom bungalow, like a doll's house. With a huge veranda. And there was a view of the lake from my bedroom. Down by the water there was a very picturesque gazebo. The town itself could have been crafted out of chocolate icing. The main drag consisted of rows and rows of tourist shops (most of them sold sailing and boating gear), which, at first, I found delightful. There weren't many ugly, boring tourists there, because it was off-season. And there were really beautiful houses down by the lake—mansions. They were so beautiful that I was already starting to have sexual fantasies about them. My fantasy was that each house had a different rich boy living inside. And someday I'd have sex with each one. Every encounter would be very romantic. Down by the boathouse with the water lapping in our ears.

The whole place just seemed filled with romantic expectation. But I was a little nervous about being around academics. Do you know what drives me crazy about most academics? They're never sure of anything. In fact, the more unsure you are about actual facts, the more intelligent you're supposed to be. Lord help you if you *assume* anything. I had this one teacher at university, her name was Lila Lamprey-Pistoli. (I've never understood the reason for hyphenated names. But just watch out for people who have them.) And she was an incredibly mean old Hungarian who was obsessed with "primary sources." You weren't allowed to take a fart unless it was from a "primary source." (In case you don't know what a primary source is, it's like—well—the original first guy or gal who said something.) Like Lila Lamprey's favourite thing to say was, "What do we know about Greek tragedy?" And then she'd answer her own question. "We know very *little* about Greek tragedy"—she just loved saying that —"because very few *primary* sources have come down to us." Secondary sources basically consisted of people guessing and making theories about things after the fact. Much more interesting reading, actually. Well, this whole negative thing about secondary sources was a big problem for me because I just love secondary sources. In fact, I love fiction, I love lies. My final M.A. project for her class was all about prostitutes in Restoration comedies. I thought these dames were really cool. It was my theory that all the actresses in Restoration comedy were hookers trying to get dates with the audience.

I didn't have a lot of proof to back it up. But I thought it was a neat theory.

Lila Lamprey didn't buy it, though. She gave me a C-minus. So it was that kind of shit that finished off academia for me. Oh, there was also the time when Lila asked me what I thought about Shaw. I said, "I don't like Shaw." She said, "I'm sorry Jack, but that's an undergraduate response." Well, fuck me, if she had waited a second I would have explained all about how Shaw is boring and cerebral and there are too many stage directions and the plays aren't even dramatic, that they're just filled with arguments. But I didn't even have a chance. She was too excited at figuring out that my response was "undergraduate."

But one thing at St. Stephen's calmed all my academic misgivings and made me forget how underqualified I was: all the attention from Matthew. Each day I'd sit in on one of his classes. He taught two courses. One in Edwardian Drama, the other a course of his own invention—The Child In Victorian and Edwardian Literature. I actually felt a bit like a little prince.

The students certainly began to notice me. Matthew very politely introduced me to the students in his two classes (saying I would be monitoring the course). But I could tell that people were impressed by our relationship. I mean, basically he was the big deal at St. Stephen's, and here I was, quickly getting a reputation for being his sidekick.

I noticed two things: first, what a good teacher Matthew was, and second, how sexually exciting the whole experience was for me.

Matthew's teaching is hard to describe because it's so organic. Sure, he could be pedantic (especially when he was alone with me), but in front of a class he was just magic. First of all, he was just so obviously very comfortable in front of a room full of people. And being so handsome and charming, it wasn't hard for people to like him. I mean, Matthew himself would be the first to admit (and I think many teachers would admit this) that students always fall in love with a good teacher. Of course, most teachers (Matthew included) make it very clear that love between a student and teacher should always be platonic. Still, Matthew admitted that a kind of idolization was definitely necessary if the students were going to learn anything. And Matthew's charm was very hard to describe, but it was all-pervasive and persuasive. He made you feel as if you were very intelligent. Students and other teachers alike. He had an intense intellectual excitement. And his teaching was wandering and unpretentious and profound. He poked and prodded at ideas until they burst open. And when they burst, he would sort of peruse the ejaculate (if I may use that term) and turn it over and taste it and eventually revel in it. You never knew how he would turn an idea. And his classroom talk seemed totally spontaneous; he made the students feel as if he were always discovering something with them.

His classes had tremendous humour. Time seemed to fly by. But he completely succeeded in drawing a fourth wall between himself and the students. He talked hypothetically, and he never revealed very much about himself. This just added to the students' love for him. The mystery became part of the idolization.

I'll have to admit I was hypnotized by this deft, handsome teacher. And I fell in love with him a little bit. But I never thought he'd go for me.

There was really only one bar in Stony Bay. (There were a couple lousy ones, actually, but there was one central bar— the real hangout.) It was called The President's Place because at one point some American president (I can't remember which one; he was really inconsequential, like Buchanan) had come to visit. It had once been a grand hotel but now it was just remodelled to look pretentious and impress the tourists. The bar staff were all fags who wouldn't admit it. And if you wanted to go out at night and have a drink and meet people, you had to go to The President's Place.

Of course, I immediately started to hang out there, because I was used to hanging out at bars in the city. And I met a young fag who ran a bookstore in town who was very charming. His name was Lyle and he was obviously HIV positive. It was obvious to me anyway, although other people might not have noticed. He was unnaturally skinny for his frame. But he was, and looked like he had always been, very beautiful. He was sitting at the bar having a little drink and we started chatting. Lyle was a Ph.D in something (I think something to do with 19th-century criminals) and he had this sort of elderly pompous way of making pronouncements about things with a faintly British accent. Even though he was clearly not British and only about thirty years old. I took to him immediately because he was, it seemed, a total slut. And he knew everything about the town and Matthew.

And he loved lecturing, in a way. He had been a teacher once, but since his diagnosis he had quit to retire early to Stony Bay. I would ask him a question, and he'd start, cigarette in one hand, and drink in the other, with his faggoty drawl. "Yes, Matthew is an odd character. He has three degrees, you know, and one of them is in science." I said I didn't know. I asked him if Matthew was involved with anyone. "No, he doesn't have a lover now. I'm sure that explains why you've been brought here." I told him I didn't have any indication that I had been "brought here" to be Matthew's lover. "I'll admit, you're an odd choice," he said. I asked him who Matthew usually went for. "Blacks," he said. I asked him if he meant Blacks from Africa or Jamaica. "No, it doesn't matter. He has something special for them. I think it's the smoothness of their skin or something—he goes on sometimes about how smooth their bodies are." This gave me the shivers because even though I was in my mid-twenties at the time, I was practically hairless and always have been. I asked him about Matthew's Black boyfriends. "Oh, there have been a few. Very beautiful Black boys. But most of them have been a little crazy—with drinking problems. Matthew, wisely, is never seen in public with them. But everyone knows that they are there. Rumour is, they piss on him." I asked him how he knew the Black boys pissed on Matthew and he said, "Everybody says so. I assume it's true." I pointed out that it could be malicious gossip. He said it was quite possible. "You know what Matthew always says." I said that I didn't. "A twitch of a curtain means a ruined reputation in this town." And I had this image all of a sudden of old millionaires' wives peering out from behind curtains, then catching a glimpse of Matthew staggering around with some drunken guy in tow, then flicking the curtains shut with a vicious, self-satisfied scowl. "It's the colonial thing with Matthew," said Lyle. "You know, he was brought up in London and that can give you a taste for the exotic."

Well, all this made Matthew more appealing suddenly. I wasn't sure, of course, if I wanted to piss on him. But he was so attractive that no fantasy was really repulsive. Besides, I've always had a thing for messing up white boys and Matthew was the whitest of them all.

Matthew had begun inviting me over to his house in the evenings to discuss his book with me. He said that he was about to start writing, and he wanted my advice. His house was just about as enchanting as everything else in Stony Bay, with four rooms around a homey country kitchen. It was a little bit faggy but not in a pretentious way. Matthew had very interesting taste in art (he had this great photograph of a hooker who had his body covered with tattoos, for instance) and lots of old furniture from his family in England, which looked very authentic. Not like, you know, "antiques."

And evenings, after the day's classes, he would have me over to dinner and he would bounce ideas off me. It was very romantic. I liked being his intellectual pillow. Sometimes he would just play his favourite music: David Del Tredici's *Alice* series. Matthew was very taken with Lewis Carroll and he loved David Del Tredici. Del Tredici is this fabulous composer who created a whole bunch of symphonies based on *Alice in Wonderland*. The symphonies are sort of wild and cacophonic and childlike. At first I didn't like them. But Matthew sort of led me, and we found beautiful melodies. Sometimes it would be a little cold and we'd light the fire and Matthew would read to me from *Alice in Wonderland*. His obsession with Lewis Carroll was all about the Victorian romanticization of repression. Matthew loved repression. As an old Brit, it kind of suited him. At the time he was—I found this out later—fifty-five years-old. But he barely looked forty-five. I guess I looked a bit like a boy to him, because I certainly only looked about twenty, even though I was over thirty. (Leave it to a couple of desperate old fags to try and pull the wool over each other's eyes about their ages.) Matthew thought that Lewis Carroll wrote *Through the Looking Glass* because of his obsession with young girls. Scholars have written a lot about this. It's old news now, of course, that Lewis Carroll loved to take pictures of naked little girls. Carroll wrote some hilarious letters to the real Alice's mother—Matthew showed them to me. Letters where he says things like "Would it be all right for me to photograph Alice in a see-through dress? I would adore so to see her delightfully curved young limbs at free play in the wind," or some such crap. Now when you read these letters, you wonder why she didn't just sock him one or send out a posse to kill him. But she did let him take lots of pictures of Alice in various states of déshabillé. There's one fabulous picture of her as this "beggar"—which was obviously a big excuse just to get Alice to look sexily sad, and to get great rips in her outfit in just the right places. Very perverted. Alice's mother did stop Alice from seeing old Lewis after the girl was about fourteen years old. But actually—and this is the really interesting part— Lewis Carroll couldn't have cared less at that point. Alice wasn't of any interest to him when she had gone as old and decrepit as fourteen. No, seriously, the guy was only interested in girls under ten. Matthew's theory was that, yes, obviously, Carroll was sexually attracted to these little girls. And Matthew thought that he would have been worth shooting, like any other garden variety pervert, except that Carroll repressed his desire and it turned into art.

He felt the same way about James Barrie, the guy who wrote *Peter Pan.* Barrie (I don't know if you're aware) was pretty seriously attracted to his neighbour's little boys. He used to hang out with them in the garden and play "innocent" games. These Victorians all get pretty spooky when they're around kids. Have you ever seen the Victorian Fairy Paintings? They had a new exhibit of these incredibly sexy Victorian paintings recently and I went to it. Wow. Those Victorians, they could justify soft-core pornography on the basis that they were "fairy" enthusiasts. (And Jesus, don't you just get tired of the whole fairy craze that's happened in the last couple of years? Fairy this and fairy that—people believing in fairies again. *Time* magazine wonders if it's a resurgence of religious faith that has caused so many people to start believing in those fucking irritating "little people" again. Maybe I resent them so much because fairies are always pictured as these sexy little molestable girls in loincloths with wings. I mean, J. M. Barrie got it right. Not many people are aware of one fact. Do you know how Tinkerbell is described in the original *Peter Pan*? Plump. She was plump, get it, Walt? Disney is such a pederastical institution. No, sorry guys, Tinkerbell isn't some fucking playboy fold-out from another world. She's supposed to be *plump*. Fat.)

Anyway, Matthew loved this whole Victorian world, because he thought repression was great, because it was, in a way, responsible for producing great art. That was Matthew's theory. And it made a lot of sense. It seemed to me that the Alice stories were filled with anger and violence and sadness. And that's what made them such great fairy tales. I mean, who wants a fairy tale where everyone is sweet and nice all the time? If you know how evil little kids are, you know that what they are looking for is some good old-fashioned violence in their reading material. But to Matthew it was pretty clear that old Lewis Carroll wouldn't have come up with such scary stuff if he hadn't repressed major feelings. I mean, anytime you repress major feelings there are major consequences.

This was where Matthew and I parted company, though. I mean, I wasn't so sure if Lewis Carroll's repression (of his sexual feelings for little girls) had any effect on his writing. See, my idea is that even though repression has heavy-duty consequences, acting out has heavy duty consequences, too. In other words, Carroll might have molested little girls, and written great stuff as well. Because basically, being a pederast (which is what were talking about here) is, by nature, sad.

And by that I don't mean to pick on pederasts. My experience with them is relatively limited. (No, I did not get molested as a child.) Everyone always thinks gay men get molested as children. Well, I didn't! And most other gay men didn't! And we're not repressing memories, or something stupid like that, we just didn't! In fact, most gay men I know wish they were molested when they were kids. Most gay men I know were lusting after their uncles, and yes, their dads, when they were eight years old. God, if someone had molested me when I was ten maybe I wouldn't have waited until I was in my late twenties to come out of the closet. I'll always remember this thing that happened when I was about sixteen. And I've seen pictures of myself when I was sixteen and I was very hot. I remember I bought a new pair of white overalls and I was sitting outside the Cineplex, waiting for a friend. And I remember some guy came up to me, trying to pick me up. I knew what he was trying to do at the time, but it was all so new to me. And I was very stupid in the sex department. So I just ignored him. Looking back, I can see I must have seemed like one hot little teenager. And I actually regret the fact that I was too dumb to pick up on his pick-up. I could have been a gay teenager, humping away. I blame the psychiatrist I had at the time.

I went to this doctor when I was sixteen years old. The reason was that I used to have anxiety attacks (about Bozo the clown and other things) and I was afraid to go out of the house. Actually, I had anxiety attacks because I had met this beautiful Italian boy named Marco. (He used to play the trumpet.) So I used to listen to Debussy's "La Mer" over and over again, waiting for the trumpet solo. It was Marco's favourite part.

And I would cry and cry. And then I would get anxious and think I was only alive if I was with Marco. Moments with Marco became the only happy moments in my life. I started to go crazy with anxiety. Well, I took all of these feelings to my therapist when I was sixteen.

He talked me out of them. He told me it was all about having separation anxiety from my mother. This was true. My mother and I were a little too close. But I eventually worked all that out and moved out of the house and learned how to say "fuck you" to her. Which was an important but traumatic experience for both of us. But I still had these homosexual feelings. The therapist encouraged me to fuck women. This, I was able to do. And I did it until I was twenty-eight. The doctor had some great theories to talk me out of being a homosexual. He asked, "How do you feel when you get these homosexual attractions?" I told him I felt all fluttery in my stomach and weak, like I was going to fall over. "You don't want to be weak, do you? You want to be strong, don't you?" Well, how was I supposed to answer a loaded question like that? I mean, obviously I wasn't going to say, "Oh yeah, I really enjoy being weak." And then I told him about having like nineteen kidney stones—I was written up in the medical journals—and the doctors had to put a tube up my penis to get them out. (I had a local anesthetic, don't worry.) Anyway, this psychiatrist got all excited about that. He said, "Don't you realize what was happening when they put a tube up your penis?" "Getting the kidney stones out?" I said, not yet catching on to his brilliant train of thought. "No, when the doctors did that, they were *fucking* you. Now you don't want to get *fucked*, do you? You want to *fuck*, don't you?"

Looking back on it, I was very lucky he didn't give me shock therapy. I've learned since that homosexuality was still considered a pathology at the time. Anyway, the upshot of all this was that I didn't have sex with another guy until I was twenty-eight. All because my therapist told me that it made me "weak" to get fucked up the ass. Who says all gay guys get fucked anyway? If you'd look at the whole thing logically, you'd realize that one guy is always doing the fucking while the other guy is not. This means that if you're gay, you could be very agressive. So much for his little "being gay is being weak" theory.

As you can see, I'm pretty pissed off that I never got to be a gay youth, that I never got seduced when I was young, and that a stupid therapist talked me out of being gay. But I will have to say that I know other gay guys who started fucking at a very early age. Some don't recommend it. That is, I know this guy who used to stand around malls when he was a teenager—wearing just a hint of makeup—and pick up older men. And he used to pick up guys in cars. He's happily married to an older guy now. But I know that because of what happened when he was a teenager he did get pretty cynical about sex. And about men in general. So there are two sides to every story.

Okay, so much for my little feelings about missing out on being a gay teen. Back to the whole pederasty thing, which is a gigantic issue. I don't think people really think about it enough. I mean, I don't know many pederasts. I only know one really registered pederast. By registered, I mean someone who goes for prepubescent types. To me, going after teenagers is not pederastical. I don't know if that's technically true. But come on. Teenagers may be confused, but they've got hard-ons all the time and they want to get laid. I know some people would say, "Just because they get hard-ons all the time doesn't mean that they should *come* all the time!" But I'm sure it's physically healthier to let it all out. And girls are the same. Anyway, I don't know what to call people who are into teenagers, but I don't think it's fair to call them pederasts. I mean, people used to get married when they were fourteen. It's only in the last hundred years that we invented something called "adolescence": the "teenager" that is always being "delinquent." In the past you were either a kid or fair game. Me? I have to admit I'm into guys that look like teenagers. But usually they have to be at least eighteen (though I did break that rule once). Yeah, I like them to look eighteen for sure. And what's the key? Hair distribution. You see, the first hair that boys get on their body is on their legs and ass and pubes. It's only later in life that they have hair on their chests and arms. So what I like is a boy-type with no chest or arm hair (or very little) but lots of hair on the butt and legs. Just this hair distribution alone, on even an older guy, can make me come in a second. In fact, the more satyr-like the better. The more half boy, half beast, the more I'm into it.

Okay, I knew one guy in the city who was a registered pederast. By that I mean that unlike me, he didn't just like young-looking guys. He liked prepubescent boys about ten or eleven years old. He used to run a bowling alley and I used to work for him. This guy gave pederasts a bad name. He was just such a horrible character. First of all, he had this booming voice. And he was one of those fags who's "onstage" all the time. You know, the type of fag who (if you're sitting in a restaurant or something) just has to talk so loud with his radio announcer's voice that everyone turns around to see what faggot is holding court. And it's not that I'm a closet case. It's just that usually the fags that talk so loud are such pretentious idiots that you don't want to hear their conversations anyway. (Not like Lyle, for instance, my HIV-positive friend. He had a theatrical drawl, but it was quiet and understated. And he was truly intelligent, so he's different.) No, this bowling alley owner was a very unattractive person and he had a Nazi-like German accent. I would come in a few minutes late for work and he'd scream at me (keep in mind, this was when someone was coming in to pick up their bowling shoes or something), "So you were out last night having a good time, were you?" That kind of thing (only it would come out more like, "So, you ver out lost nit haffing a gut time, ver you?"). And because he ran a bowling alley, he had all these great video and pinball games, and he was a video and pinball game expert. (Most pederastical types are experts at video games and pinball.) Pretty young things would come in to play the hot new video games at the bowling alley, and he'd eye them, then draw them aside. I'd hear him (with his booming Nazi voice) saying, "Yass, I know the man who invented thiss gahm, he's a virry smaaat men, vood you lick me to introduss you to him?" And the kid would be looking up at this guy—who was blubbery fat, bald, and very unattractive, by the way—and the next thing you know the owner of the bowling alley would be in back blowing this kid while I was handing out smelly shoes. It was humiliating. I finally had to quit: I was tired of working the counter while he was fucking young boys. And I was tired of him. He struck me as the kind of person who couldn't possibly have a sexual relationship with an adult. First of all, he was dreadfully unattractive (but people do triumph over that, I know). And secondly, he was such a pretentious nerd (his speciality was video games, for Chrissakes!) that any intelligent adult would see through him. Finally, he was so prone to temper tantrums that if you had any life experience at all you'd just say to yourself, "I don't have to put up with this," and dump him. But to some dumb kid, yeah, he might be very impressive.

On the other hand, I wouldn't go on record as saying that these kids were that much worse off for getting blown by this loud Nazi-like fatbar. I mean, what would it hurt? It wasn't going to make them gay. If they were straight, they certainly wouldn't let the old pervert talk them into it. And if they were just interested, it would certainly take them to the next step. And if they were gay, it would at least be a non-abusive first experience. (Nobody hit anybody or anything. And he didn't tie them up.)

This bowling alley owner also had a friend who was this ancient pederast who hobbled down the bowling alley stairs with a cane. Apparentlly he liked 'em really young. Again, he seemed like a bit of a social misfit (and I found him totally disgusting), so these two guys were not, for me anyway, a great introduction to the world of pederasty.

I saw this movie once, called *Chickenhawk*, which is the best movie ever. It's all about pederasts, guys who are into young boys. And the main thing I can say about these guys is they really remind me of Lewis Carroll. Really sad. I mean, there's this one guy in *Chickenhawk* who is especially repulsive (I think all movies should be about repulsive people up close—those are my favourite kinds of movies) because he is very chubby-cheeked and eager and piglike. (I don't want to give you the idea that *all* pederasts are ugly, sad, piglike Nazis. I've actually met some very attractive happy-type guys who are into Italian boys or skateboarders. Some of these attractive pederasts dress up like kids, and they're so cute that you can't tell them from the teenagers. The young-looking, attractive pederasts can get weary of the whole game, though. If you're going to pick up a kid, you have learn to talk the way a kid talks. So unless you're actually into video games and rap music, it can get tiresome. No matter how horny you are. A lot of pederasts are actually very happy, living in Morocco. Apparently, in Morocco the mothers regularly walk by your house and offer to sell you their kids, which I guess to a pederast is like dying and going to heaven. I also knew this one guy who used to run an antique store—he practically started the whole gay liberation movement in my city. Sometimes it's the pederasts that are the most political fags. Political, in a good way.) Anyway, there's this scene in *Chickenhawk* where the old hawk drives past a mall and there are a bunch of kids playing pinball (I'll admit, the kids are very beautiful, even for someone like me who likes them more legal) and he very shyly chats them up. That's it. It's over in a matter of minutes, and he just chats with them, that's all. So then he gets back into the car. And the old chickenhawk says to the interviewer, "Wow, he really likes me, he really likes me, did you see the way that kid looked at me—seductive, oh so seductive. Yes, he was really flirting with me. He really wants me, oh yes, oh yes." Practically salivating all over the microphone. And, of course, to an outsider (and to the kid he was flirting with, probably) the kid was just playing pinball and this old guy was just passing the time with him. And that's what seems so sad about these guys. They seem to be making something out of nothing. I mean, the kid was just being nice by talking to him. And this old guy is all "Oh he wants me, he wants me."

But, of course, after I saw the movie and sat around feeling superior to this old chickenhawk for a while, thinking he was a lot sadder than me, I began to think of my own life. And the lives of a lot of my friends.

I know a lot of married straight women. Now, their husbands are such unfeeling pigs that the most affectionate thing they might do is pat them on the butt after tossing the Frisbee. You know the kind of asshole I mean. And a lot of these straight husbands don't even fuck their wives. What I'm trying to say is this: it's true that these chickenhawks just seem to be making a lot out of nothing. They seem to be exaggerating the crumbs of affection or even attention they get from their so-called loved ones. But then again, isn't that what love is? Isn't that what defines mad, true love? Being obsessed and satisfied with shreds of nothing from the beloved? Isn't pederasty then, in a way, the love in our culture that is most like the kind of "true" love in storybooks?

For instance, old Bill Yeats used to be in love with actress Maude Gonne. Why? Because she lived up to her name. She was gone all the time (off in France somewhere). She was untouchable, unreachable. Just like these boys who will always grow up, always leave. If you can get over being uptight about this pederasty stuff, I think you can see that, in a way, being a pederast is like being in a storybook romance.

If you're looking for other movies on pederastical subjects, Hollywood offers one or two great choices. Of course, there's the obvious, the recently released *Happiness*, which is this avant-garde type of film about a married child molester. I guess it's pretty realistic about the problems that a guy might have if he has a sexual desire for his own son. But again, it sure paints a pretty sad picture of pedophiles. What I mean is, the last scene (which is so sad that it's hard to watch, and if a movie is hard to watch, it's a good movie in my books. I've never been able to watch the last scene in Pasolini's *Salo*, which makes it a masterpiece as far as I'm concerned!) where the boy asks the father, "Would you ever want to have sex with me?"—it's just scary as hell. They're both crying and it's just so pitiful. But I can't help thinking: hey, don't any straight fathers ever desire their daughters? Of course they do. Like everyday! I'm sure straight fathers must go and wank off in a corner sometimes dreaming about fucking their daughters. What I'm trying to say is that *Happiness* (it's by Todd Solondz, and I'm sure you can get it at the video store) is a great movie because there are lots of close-ups of ugly people in it, and close-ups of ugly people make the greatest movies. And I mean, couldn't even a closeted, gay child molester have, like, one or two happy moments in his life? Would his whole life have to be dismal? That's Hollywood for you.

The best pederastical movie in the whole world is called *Apt Pupil*. As usual, of course, the producers of this stupid but fabulous movie actually have no idea that they''ve made a pederastical classic. That, in my opinion, is when Hollywood is at its best, actually. When they make a movie that's supposed to be a frightening analysis of Nazism and it just turns out to be a great wankoff for old guys who love boys. When Hollywood is trying very hard to be virtuous and intellectual, you can bet that the movie will turn out to be really dirty. It's just a law of human nature, really. Set out to be the nicest, most god-fearing person in the world and you'll find yourself jerking off underneath subway grates, staring up little girls' dresses.

Anyway, *Apt Pupil* stars Ian McKellan, who is like the only real "out" homosexual actor in the world. So that says something. If Ian McKellan is willing to act in a movie nowadays there's usually some sort of homosexual aspect to the film, because he's the only big actor that ever lived that didn't need a case of AIDS to bring him out of the closet. (I guess there's Rupert Everett, too, but Ian gets more points because he was such an old, venerable, respected codger when he *did* come out.) I remember seeing the trailers for *Apt Pupil* and anticipating a wankfest. There was old Ian looking kind of sharp, actually, in his Nazi uniform, and there was Brad Renfro, some kid actor from TV, just barely a teenager, looking so beautiful you just wanted to kiss him and then come on his face. Well, the movie is about the friendship between a very cute boy and an old Nazi. The nature of their relationship is very confusing. The boy is sort of obsessed with nighttime dreams of Nazis, which sort of resemble AIDS night sweats. But who cares anyway, because he goes to sleep wearing only underwear (What cute little tits! What a muscled stomach!) and then wakes up all delectable and sweaty, panting into the camera. Another great erection moment comes when Brad Renfro (feeling frisky one day, I guess) asks old Ian M. to dress up like a Nazi and march around for him. This is the kinkiest thing I've seen in a mainstream movie in years. Old guys dressing up in uniforms for young guys? It's usually the other way around. But hey, a change is as good as a rest. Then there's a great scene where the two of them have some sort of movie-manipulated confrontation and old Ian looks down on pitiful, fuckable little Brad and says, "You know we're fucking each other right now. You know that, don't you?" Or something like that.

(Oh, I forgot to tell you about the greatest, most kitschy pederastical scene in the movie. Brad Renfro is taking a shower at school after a basketball game—a unique opportunity for the director to show lots of hot, naked, young guys taking showers. And Brad is just sort of showering, looking gorgeous and glancing around at all the pretty boys showering around him—like guys always do in showers. Then suddenly Brad throws his head back and there's a fantasy sequence where all the beautiful showering boys suddenly morph into ugly, old men. It's supposed to be a nightmarish concentration camp moment, but it just reminded me of a bad night at The Baths.)

As you can see, people get to watch all this soft-core pornography while at the same time congratulating themselves that they're getting an education about the evils of Nazism. It's fun seeing evil up close, it can even give you a hard-on! The scene that proves to me that the movie is just full of shit (in a great way) is where Ian McKellan tries to put a cat in the oven. Just to prove how evil Nazis are, ol' Ian is just sitting in his suburban backyard one summer night, smoking some of his skanky-looking Nazi cigarettes, when he spies a sweet old ginger pussy sitting on a chair. So Nazi Ian goes, "Hmmm. What could be more fun than torturing that old ginger cat?" (He doesn't actually say this, but it's what he's thinking.) Then he picks up the pretty ol' cat and takes her into the kitchen. Then he opens the oven and turns it on. And we're thinking: no, no, this is too much, I can't believe he's actually going to stick that pretty old pussy who never hurt anybody into the stove! Well, sure enough he tries to stuff the cat, kicking and hissing, into the oven. It's actually a harrowing moment. (The kitty does get away, in case you're a member of PETA.) But come on, this incident is not even factually accurate! I mean, as far as I know, one thing that all Fascists have in common is that they love animals. (Hitler and Stalin loved dogs, and Nixon had Checkers.) But of course, in a stupid movie like this, Nazis just go around torturing animals for fun in their spare time.

I know I've gone off on a tangent here. And it all started with Lewis Carroll. But I'm just trying to make you understand an issue that became a major difference of opinion between Matthew and I. It shaped my whole experience at St. Stephen's.

Earlier I said that I noticed what a good teacher Matthew was, and also how sexually exciting the experience was for me. Well, I didn't really explain the "sexually exciting" part.

Yes, it's true. What was going on from the moment I started at St. Stephen's was more than just being excited about my little doll's house by the lake. And more than being a little in love with this dapper dean. It was also that I was very sexually excited by the students. The male students, to be exact. It was something I had known would be a bit of an issue, but something I hadn't wanted to deal with. (Teaching, after all, was going to be my new career—my new way of making money, anyway.) But I knew very well that my attraction was mainly for younger men with a certain hair distribution. And I was very aware that a lot of the students walking around this university had very hairy legs, and hairy butts, and no hair on their chest at all, and probably a thin little treeline of fur on their flat stomachs leading directly down to their pubes. I mean, all of this exciting body hair was having a party under their clothes.

I was very attracted to the kids. And I wasn't quite sure what I was going to do about it. At first it wasn't so bad, because I was falling in love with Matthew, but later it got worse.

So when Matthew and I talked about Lewis Carroll, we were talking (in a sort of veiled way) about dealing with our mutual attraction to the students. How we both might manage to deal with that issue. And so the argument could become quite volatile (but still sexy, in a Katherine Hepburn/Spencer Tracy sort of way). You see, I certainly mentioned to Matthew that some of the students were beautiful. And he mentioned it to me. And Matthew always made it very clear that it was all right to notice the beauty of a student, to even obsess over it. But it would never be right to act. And all this fit with his theories about Lewis Carroll. Because Matthew believed that what made Carroll's art great was the artist's repression. And he believed what made a great teacher was this attraction to the students, being in love with the students even, in a way, but *never* acting upon it. This is what made the whole thing a "mission." I think he picked his teachers for this reason. Most of the male teachers were, I thought, closeted homosexuals. Teaching, after all, is a profession that attracts closeted fags. Like monks. But sometimes there is a power overflow, a blowout. And then, of course, some closet case is caught wanking with dirty magazines or kills himself or something. So far, nothing like that had happened at St. Stephen's. Everyone seemed to just love the whole repression thing. I'm not completely knocking repression. I have a theory that the greatest art—in western culture anyway—comes from oppressed peoples. But I don't think you have to go out and get all repressed just to produce art. I think you can just look out at the sunset and think, "Oh, I'm so little and inconsequential, and soon I'll be dead, and who could give a fuck really, except my cat." Art usually hits you on the head at a time like that. I will admit that I sort of acquiesced to Matthew when we argued about this. I was kind of acting the part of the student. After all, I wanted him to kiss me. (That's all I really wanted, in fact, was for him to kiss me—I wanted it so bad!)

So, like Katherine Hepburn with old Spencer Tracy, I let him win. I said, "You may be right, Matthew," when he said that teachers should never sleep with students. After all, at the time it made sense. And deep down, Matthew was pretty conservative. I think it all comes from being an old Brit. I mean, to his mother, or some straight old lady, I'm sure he might seem outrageous. But to me, he was a British school-boy gone bad. Someone who was being "naughty" all the time. I don't know if you've ever been to London, but the place is obsessed with being naughty. I used to have a boyfriend once who was a hooker in England, and he said there was a lot of money to be made from spanking. I mean, he made a living for a year just spanking these old coots. If you go to any phone booth in London, you see all these ads for "naughty spankings" and "I'm a bad schoolgirl, correct me!" and stuff like that. I swear that if English people just stopped capital punishment in school, there would be no business for the prostitution industry. Now, Matthew wasn't into spanking or anything. But there was something about the way he made love that made me imagine he thought the whole thing was naughty.

But I'll get to that in a minute.

I mean, this whole naughty business fit right in with Matthew's views about AIDS. I remember he said, "You know what's the cause of all this AIDS business, don't you?" And I said, "No." And he said, "You know, those fellows in San Francisco, putting their fists up each other's rectums, ten times a night." I said, "Yes." (Though I never would have called these freaks *fellows*, or their messy a-holes *rectums*.) "Well, that's going too far. That's going beyond the limit. You see, the human body can't stand it." As you can see, Matthew often spoke as if he was teaching. Everything to him was a lesson, and I'd nod and say yes, most of the time, even though I'd be thinking, right. The limit. I get it. So fisting ten times a night is the limit.

Does that mean it's okay if you do it just nine times? Because my whole theory about AIDS is that nobody really knows what causes it. I mean, don't get me wrong, I think condoms are a good idea. But as far as I can tell, nobody really knows what actually causes AIDS. Or how to cure it. I mean, just use your common sense. If the medical establishment knew what caused it, they would cure it, right? (*If* anybody in the medical establishment wants to cure it. They sure make a lot of money selling drugs that make you sicker, though. That's a whole other issue.) Anyway, you can be sure that all these "limits" that people talk about when they're talking about AIDS basically have to do with what people find sexually disgusting. For instance, I'm quite into rimming (which, for you stupid people who never get out of your houses, is sucking ass). And once I read this AIDS pamphlet that said rimming was dangerous. I couldn't believe it. I just couldn't get the science of it. AIDS is supposed to be spread by blood and semen, neither of which is going on in rimming. Well, I asked my doctor at the time, who was one of the major AIDS doctors in the world (I figured it was a good idea, if you're a fag, to get a good AIDS doctor) about this whole rimming business. He agreed with me. I said, "Don't you think that rimming is just a danger for hepatitis and parasites, not AIDS? And don't you think that the reason people say that rimming is a risk for AIDS is because they just want to stop people from doing it? Because, basically, most people find rimming disgusting?" And he said, "Yes." And he was straight. A real nice guy, though.

But for Matthew, this whole concept of "we've gone too far" was very attractive. So when he'd talk about it, I'd agree.

I hope you don't think I was horrible for letting Matthew win arguments just so he would fall in love with me.

I looked at it very practically. Matthew is a teacher. I'm a bit too old to be his student, but I can make him feel that I am his student if I just allow him to win all the arguments. Not that Matthew was stupid. That's what made it so interesting. Actually, I agreed with him most of the time—which made it easy. But now and then, on crucial issues, like whether or not people had innate sexual "limits" or whether or not students should fuck teachers, I'd acquiesce. Which wasn't lying. Let's face it, lots of women do it all the time with straight men. Because straight men have such fragile egos. And if you don't tell them that they're right all the time then they can't get hard-ons anymore. That's what straight women tell me about straight men, anyway.

So you may be thinking two things about all this. First of all, isn't it sort of a contradiction that Matthew thought teachers shouldn't fuck students, and yet here I had to act like his student to get him to fuck me? Well, yes, I'd say, that's a contradiction. That was, to me, the ultimate hypocrisy of Matthew: "Never, ever, under any circumstances, should you touch a student in a sexual or romantic way, but hey, let me be your moral and intellectual and personal teacher, and then I'll feel attracted to you." Of course, I could never point this out to him. That would make *me* the teacher and less sexually attractive.

Secondly—you might be thinking—was it opportunistic and sleazy of me to pretend to be Matthew's student? Wasn't it just to get a job at St. Stephen's? No, that's not what I was doing. I already had the job at St. Stephen's. (He was going to start me in January, in the winter semester.) No, I was in love with Matthew. And I was actually learning stuff from him. Stuff he didn't even know he was teaching me.

So anyway, *finally*, Matthew asked me to have sex with him. I mean, I must have gone to his house every other night for a month without him asking me. The sexual tension around his cozy little fire was palpable. And I was pondering, should I make a move? We spend so much time together, and we're both attractive, and attracted to each other, and we have so much in common, so like, when? Actually, it went on for so long without sex, or kissing, or anything romantic, that I thought it might never happen. And I would always go back to my little doll's house by the lake sheepishly wondering: when?

Then one night, we were actually sitting on the couch together. He was reading from *Through the Looking Glass* and explaining some Lewis Carroll mathematical thing to me. Suddenly he closed the book and said, "When are we going to sleep together, anyway?" It seemed like a very British and polite question, coming from him. I was taken completely off guard. But I knew my answer. "What about tonight?" I said.

It was the way he said it—sort of offhand—as if it was just the most natural thing in the world. And it would just be so fucking foolish if we didn't. And I had to agree.

So sleeping with Matthew was a weird but beautiful thing. He had poppers, which I loved. I remember he kept poppers and lube in a little straw box under the bed. And he was mainly into jerking off. He said he never went in for "anal sex." Well, that was fine with me. I had no desire to lick his ass. I just wanted to kiss that beautiful face.

I don't know if I can describe Matthew's face. I know I said he looked like Paul Newman. His lips were very straight but full. Luscious, in a controlled way. His eyes were steely blue, his nose was straight, and he had lovely cheekbones. He gave me a photo of himself as a young man. It was a beautiful picture, from some 1960s photographer in Seattle. He was wearing a suit and tie. He said, "If only we had met when I looked like that."

But it didn't matter to me that he was older. He probably would have scared the shit out of me if he had been that beautiful and young. So basically, we would lie in bed and kiss and jack off and take poppers and listen to David Del Tredici or Philip Glass. It was very romantic. And Matthew and I were usually drunk and stoned.

That was another thing about him that made me think that he was like a naughty schoolboy. He would only have sex when he was completely "out of it." Actually, he was a functioning alcoholic, which was great. I was always amazed at how smashed he could get and still do it. And then he'd wake up the next morning and be this brilliant teacher. He got smashed every night, but he got up every morning. Quick, and bright as a penny. Some nights, I will admit, we didn't have sex once we got started. Sometimes we would just hug (which was fine with me). And usually after I came (I usually came first) he'd start laughing in this weird, uncontrolled sort of school-boy way. It was very strange; un-teacherlike, but invigorating. I loved to see him release like that. And he liked the way I made lots of noise when I came. Oh yeah, I forgot to tell you that. I yell and scream and just generally wake the neighbours when I orgasm. Well, for this old Brit my screams were liberating. We just loved kissing and jerking off. He told me I was pantherlike, smooth, graceful. And when I was in bed with him, my teacher, my mentor—and I guess you could say, my dad—I was.

In fact, sometimes the sheer dadlike brilliance of him would be a technique I used to make myself come. Sometimes, if we were both really drunk (or, whatever, you know, it happens sometimes) the spunk was stubborn and wouldn't rise. When this happened, I would just fixate on the way those beautiful students (mostly the boys, of course) idolized Matthew. And I would think about how they wanted to be sucking his cock, like I was doing. And that would make me come. Sometimes I would think of how respected and well-known Matthew was. And I would think of what a privilege it was to be sucking his cock. (I will admit, on desperate nights, I would use the Arab Slave Boy Fantasy. This fantasy was all about being tied up and made to sit on this rotating wheel. In the dream, I'm an Arab slave boy and the wheel has different dildos attached to every spoke. And each dildo gets bigger and bigger as the wheel turns. And I'm forced to sit on each dildo until finally I have to sit on an emormous one—don't even ask me how big!) When I was really desperate, I thought about *The Dead Poets Society*.

It's one of my favourite movies, I'm sure you've seen it. And it's very gay. Robin Williams is not the most attractive person (too hairy for me), but his relationship with the boys is definitely homoerotic. I mean, the movie tries to dispel all this homoerotic stuff (the way Hollywood movies always do) by actually joking about it. At one point, Robin Williams (the teacher) is telling Ethan Hawke (so yummy and vulnerable) about his days as a "youth," and about how he used to go into the woods with his male student friends and read poetry. Williams says, "We weren't a Greek organization." In other words, "We weren't fags!" Yeah, I'll bet. And when Robin Williams's own students (who are all fucking gorgeous) take his suggestion and go off into the cave to read poetry together (pardon me, but no straight boys would ever do that, ever), they never do anything remotely bad. They drink and they dress up funny and invite dumb girls to watch (not that girls are generally dumb, but these are actually two dumb ones). I mean, my adolescent fantasies went way further than anything that these guys do in the cave. They don't even circle jerk. (Did anybody circle jerk? That's one question I'd like answered right now. I've heard about circle jerks, read about circle jerks, but I've never been to one. Except a hokey one that was set up by an adult gay jerkoff club, but that doesn't count. Do circle jerks really exist? Did you ever get involved in one when you were a kid? How many were in the circle? Did people come?)

But it wasn't those hokey cave scenes from *Dead Poets* that would get me an orgasm. I would think of Matthew as Robin Williams (only more cute and less hairy, because he was), and I'd think of when Robin Williams quotes Walt Whitman. (Walt Whitman for Chrissakes!—the gayest American who ever lived!)

Maybe the poem where Whitman says, "O Captain, My Captain!" Sometimes, when I was jerking off with Matthew, I would whisper in his ear, "O Captain, My Captain!" and I would come immediately. I think he was too drunk to hear it, usually.

By the way, if you fell in love with Ethan Hawke—who played a sexy student in *Dead Poet's Society*—then you can see him grow bigger and even more beautiful—a rare thing in film—in *Gattaca*. If you're like me, you've accepted the fact that Hollywood movies are not about characters, they're about actors. Let's face it, when we go to see an Ethan Hawke movie, we don't go to see the new character he's playing, we go to find out "Hey, what's Ethan Hawke up to now?" That's what Hollywood's really about.

I have a very special relationship with Ethan Hawke, actually. I sat beside him in a restaurant once. I was in New York City in Greenwich Village, having breakfast at this little outdoor café, (I can usually only afford to stay in New York City for one day, so I try and make as much of it as possible), and who should sit down beside me? Ethan. I saw Robert Sean Leonard first, if you can believe it. And Robert Sean Leonard is like my total jerkoff teen idol; he was in *Dead Poets Society* also. He plays the skinny boy with one big eyebrow who wants to act the part of some fairy in a student production of *Midsummer Night's Dream*. But his father won't let him. His ambition thwarted, he commits suicide. What could be gayer than that? Anyway, first of all I see Robert Sean Leonard, only this is like ten years after the movie was made. So he's older. But he still looks like Robert Sean. Still one eyebrow. And I'm absolutely captivated-in-love. Initially, I can't remember where I know him from. But I just know he's some kind of teen idol. And with him is a nerdy guy with a dog. The guy has patchy, icky facial hair, and he's short and wearing baggy clothes. I think at first he's just some hanger-on to Robert Sean. And then they sit down right beside me, and the short nerd with icky facial hair starts talking about Uma. Yeah, *Uma*. The icky nerd talks in a very loud voice and says things like, "Well, you know, Uma is very cranky because the baby is late and we had this huge argument and, you know, we don't want to induce early delivery because that's not a great thing to do. Well, the fight had to do with my mother, because Uma and my mother don't get along. They never have. My mother can be very, well, she and Uma, you know." It seemed to me that every time he said the word "Uma" he kind of punched it like a big beach ball, so that everyone would be sure to hear. So I started thinking, and it didn't take me long, how many Umas are there in the world? He's obviously talking about Uma Thurman! And since Ethan Hawke is married to Uma Thurman—well then, the little nerd with icky facial hair is obviously Ethan Hawke! And he's going on and on about his mother who lives in Woodstock and who used to know Timothy Leary. In a really loud voice, actually. Anyway, it just strikes me that he's so short, and not half as attractive as you'd expect. This always happens with big stars. I sat next to Liza Minelli once, in similar circumstances, and she's also incredibly short. Anyway, the next thing that strikes me is, well, why is he talking so loud about Uma in a public place? I really mulled this part over, because I do idolize Ethan Hawke—for having such a flat, muscled tummy, if nothing else—and I didn't want to think he was an asshole. But I couldn't figure out why a big movie star would sit in a street café on one of the busiest streets in the world and talk about his famous wife and all the details of their personal life in such a loud voice. And then he started to try and bully Robert Sean Leonard into being in this play with him out in Woodstock. And it all became clear. Ethan Hawke *is* kind of an asshole. You should have heard him! He was saying stuff like, "I found this rehearsal hall in Woodstock and I think they'd be willing to let us use it for cheap, and I thought we could go out there and work on some Beckett." That's what he said, I'm not kidding you. He didn't say *Happy Days* or *Waiting for Godot* but "some Beckett." As if Samuel Beckett were some goddamn intellectual bargain vegetable, like sliced carrots or pickled celery. "And you know, I don't think we need a director," he continued.

Robert Sean Leonard didn't seem too impressed by the idea. But Ethan Hawke wouldn't let him talk. He just kept saying things like, "You know, we can do some great stuff, just fooling around ourselves. I think it could be very creative. Of course, we could get a director, of course, we could get Sam—you know, Sam Shepherd, and he'd be great, but do we really want a director?" At this point I almost choked on my sunny side ups! Imagine, the arrogance of some Hollywood actor thinking he and his friends could do any productive work on "some Beckett" without a director. And then just the nauseous name dropping—"Sam, you know, Sam Shepherd." I couldn't stand it. It was so obvious that Ethan was in that café, in New York, dropping names, because he wanted everyone to know that he was a serious actor. I mean, why else would a Hollywood actor sit in a grungy Greenwich Village café and talk about Beckett? Because he wants to be taken seriously. It was all very sad, actually. And I thought of poor Uma at home having to deal with Ethan's mother, who, if she was half as selfish and obnoxious as him, must have been a real handful. But when I look back on it, I still think Ethan Hawke is gorgeous. And I still think I'd like to jerk off and then come on his perfect stomach someday. Which just goes to show what a contradictory relationship we have with our Hollywood idols.

Anyway, one way or another, Matthew and I had a great sex life. Don't get me wrong, I wasn't using The Arab Slave Boy fantasy (or Robin Williams/Ethan Hawke fantasies) all the time. Most of the time it was just Matthew's gentle but slightly rough beard, the flush and the arch of his cheekbone when he was horny, and his piercing blue eyes that made me come.

But I'll have to admit, once I get down to it, that the real aphrodisiac (the thing that kept me going, besides his sheer charm and beauty) was the whole dad thing. I mean, when I was fucking Matthew I was fucking my father, or the dad I never had, or something. I say that because I think it's a very important part of gay sex. I don't know if you're aware of it, but Puerto Rican guys, when they get fucked, apparently always say, "Papi, Papi." That means: Daddy, Daddy. Now some people might assume from this that all Puerto Ricans are molested by their fathers. But I think it's more likely that they're just being honest about a cultural thing. I'm sure a lot of straight guys yell out, "Oh, Mommy!" or something like that when they're coming. Hey, don't straight guys look at big women sometimes and say, "Come to me, momma!" when they want to fuck them? I think most times when people are having sex, one person is the parent and the other is the child. And that may vary with the act, or with the mood, or with the night, or whatever. But it's certainly part of it. And with us, Matthew was Dad: my intellectual protector. I'd quite simply never met anybody smarter than me who wanted me. (I know that sounds very conceited, but that's how I felt.)

So Matthew and I started fucking when I started teaching. And it continued on into the spring. I will admit, I did have to get rid of this other guy in his life, though. Alistair.

Alistair was this smarmy little administrative assistant of Frank's. He was taking some courses at St. Stephen's on the side and he wanted to be a teacher someday. He was quite cute in a little-boy way (except that he wasn't a little boy, he was at least thirty). I had heard rumours about Alistair, just like I heard rumours about Matthew's Black guys, and both rumours turned out to be true. I asked Matthew, for instance, if he had been attracted to Black guys, and he said, "Yes." I also asked him if the Black boys ever pissed on him and he said, "No." He actually thought it was very funny that people gossiped about him. I think he was flattered in an uptight old Brit sort of way. And then I asked him if my hairless legs were like Black guys' legs and he said, "Yes." You know, I guess it would be the same for men who like women with hair on their arms. Then, you see, that fetish would attract them to Italian women (since Italian women are, for the most part, hairy).

And listen, don't accuse me of racism about this. If you have any knowledge of human desire at all, you'll know that sexual attraction sometimes is based on race—which is really just an extension of the concept of "physical type." Now, I will admit I find it annoying when I'm trying to make someone (at a party, for instance) and I find out they only sleep with Black men. Some queens are just so completely intense about the whole thing. They won't even talk to white people. I mean, I know some Rice Queens—sorry, it's the gay terminology, even Asian men use the term—that get so squirrelly when Asian men are around that they won't even bother to talk to big white guys like me. I guess my only problem with fetishizing race is that people get so single-minded about it that they get rude at parties. But that goes for any fetish, really.

And Matthew told me about how some of his Black guys had been drunks. (Now, not all Black boys are drunks; it's just that Matthew, again, had a fetish for that kind.) And he'd had to keep them quiet around Stony Bay. In fact, Matthew was very clear about the etiquette. About me and Stony Bay, for instance. He said, "I will never walk with you around Stony Bay. We won't be going for walks together." Okay, no big deal. "Even when it's dark?" I asked. "No," he said. "Not even when it's dark." So I just figured it was one of those relationship restrictions you live with. Matthew had another one. "I don't call. I never call. You can call me. But I won't ever call you on the telephone." Okay. You don't like phones. Fine with me. I really didn't mind these restrictions.

But I did mind Alistair. It wasn't so much that I was jealous. Or maybe I was. Yeah, I guess I was. Alistair was a little suck, very sweet and cheerful and pretty. Everything I was not. But the main reason I hated him was not because he was fucking Matthew when I started fucking Matthew. No, I can be very open-minded about things like that. Honestly. It's one of the great things about being gay. You can kind of *not* be jealous sometimes. I mean, if Alistair had been this beautiful boy (a real boy, not a fake one) then I probably would have been jealous. But I also would have been forgiving. I would have thought: I love Matthew and this is good for him. No, really. This is something that straight people don't understand. They sure do understand moralism, though. "Eat your beets, they're good for you." (Something straight people say a lot, in one way or another, in my experience.) Well, sometimes a beautiful boy is good for you, and you should fuck him for your general health.

But not Alistair. Alistair was bad for Matthew because, first of all, he wasn't actually having sex with Matthew. He was almost having sex with him, cockteasing him. He would sleep in Matthew's bed, if you can believe it, but Matthew was not allowed to touch him. Well, when I heard this, I put my foot down. Teacher or no teacher, daddy or no daddy, I wasn't standing for this from him. "He doesn't have sex with you?" I asked. "No, but he lets me lie with him." "He *lets* you *lie* with him?" I was furious. Oh, I was mad. "He's not half as cute as you, that's ridiculous. Don't sleep with him anymore, he's a creep," I wanted to say, "and he's using you to get out of the administration biz and get a job at St. Stephen's!" But I knew it would hurt Matthew. So I didn't say it. Anyway, I got my way. Matthew was sleeping with me too much of the goddamn time; he had nothing left for Alistair.

So it was kind of our little honeymoon in Stony Bay. At the

bar, I told my new friend Lyle that I was sleeping with Matthew. "I had a feeling that was going to happen," said Lyle. "So, does he like to piss on you?" he asked airily. "No, that was just a rumour," I said. "He says I have legs like a Black boy, though." "How wonderful for both of you," said Lyle, and I could tell that behind his sarcasm was a little bit of sweetness. "I will have to admit I'm disappointed. Great men usually have their sexual quirks, and without one, I don't know if Matthew is really a great man." "He does poppers and only likes to jerk off," I informed him. "Like every other fag in the world," said Lyle. "You know, speaking of famous folk and their sexual pecadillos, I was quite excited to learn that Pasolini liked to be shat upon." "Oh, did he?" I inquired, being quite a Pasolini fan. (This detail only energized my interest.) "Oh yes." Lyle was in his element. "His big thing was to pick up some nice, meaty, Italian peasant type, feed him pizza, and then have the boy shit on him." "That's fascinating," I said. "Well," I continued, "think of all the shit imagery in his movies. Like, in *Canterbury Tales*—the giant asses that shit out monks." "In *Salo* they eat shit," said Lyle. "Oh, I could never watch that movie," I said, which was true. "Oh, you should, it's great, the most horrifying movie I've ever seen!" said Lyle. And then we had a big discussion about directors and their weird sexual proclivities. We both believed that Roman Polanski was a great guy. And the girl he molested was certainly old enough to know better at the time. After all, she would have been marrying age in Bali. And then we bonded over a very important principle. All the critics who say that Woody Allen's marriage to Soon-yi has ruined his movies should be shot. I mean, give me a break. It certainly doesn't sound like a very healthy relationship for either of them, but does that mean his movies aren't funny? "I'm sorry, I just can't find Woody Allen's movies funny anymore since he married his adopted daughter." We laughed a lot over that one.

I thought it was a good idea to keep up my friendships.

Because you never know how long gay love affairs will last.

And in January, I started my own teaching.

It was very interesting. I mean, I think in some ways I'm a born teacher. Teaching is a lot like acting, performing. You're up in front of a room full of people and you've got to come up with something. If it's all just information, then people are going to get bored very quickly. So I liked the performance part of it. And I'm a great talker (as you can probably tell). I can go on and on about almost anything (and nothing). The first classes I taught were "directing for the theatre" classes. One was for beginners and the other was for more advanced students. I have to admit I was sort of hoping some of my students would be attractive. But, you know, almost none of them were. Maybe it was because Matthew was at the centre of my attention at the time. Or maybe it was my nervousness about teaching. But most of my students were duds. Most of them were girls, in fact. My big problem was remembering their names. All the girls looked alike to me. The only way I could remember them was by hairdos. And the thing about teenage girls is that they change their hairdos and their hair colour, like, twice a day. I had this pair of girls named Tiffany and Tolly. I shouldn't call them a pair, they weren't a pair at all. They were separate human beings in their own right who just had the misfortune to end up in my class. And have similar, white, boring names. I could not get them sorted out. And they were both equally as lazy and sheepish and annoying. I even did that exercise where every time you call on somebody you say their name. "Yes, Tiffany," I would say. Only it would be Tolly. They got hurt (the way teenage girls do) but I was really trying my best, I was.

The boys were a different matter. I could tell *them* apart. They were all just as unnattractive, though. Except for this one boy whose name was David Lovejoy. I'm serious, Lovejoy. He was sort of short and chunky. He looked like one of my ex-boyfriends. So this sort of sparked me. And I was convinced that he was flirting with me, completely convinced of it. Which I realize is totally normal. Students do it all the time and probably don't even know they're doing it. He would actually say things like, "Well, Jack, a big attractive guy like you," in the middle of class. Things like that. I just ignored him. And there were lots of couches in the class because it was a directing class. So sometimes he would just curl up on a couch all cozy, like a little baby or something. I found all this very attractive. But it didn't torture me or anything. I just mentally observed, "Oh, that's interesting. Some of the students will flirt with me. Well, thank heavens they're not that attractive and I'm having lots of sex with Matthew." It didn't faze me.

I also made friends with this great professor named Pat. She's kind of hard to describe except that she's sort of a straight woman living in a lesbian's body. If that makes any sense. Basically, she's extremely short and angular (almost midget size) with a butch haircut. And there's something very butch about her. She's definitely a dominant type. And she enjoyed torturing her students. I got to know her very quickly because she was very friendly over the photocopier. She was unbelievably intelligent and she was tenured. And a Ph.D. So it was nice of her to chum around with a veritable plebe like me. Even though I'll admit it did up my status a bit to be sleeping with the dean!

Torturing students was something that she did with a lot of affection. Some kid would come in and ask for an extension on a paper, say. And she'd be like, "No." And they'd do the pleading and whining and stuff. And she'd just go, "No." And then they'd whine some more. And she'd say, "Sorry, the paper is due one day earlier." I couldn't believe it. It was just punishment for having been such a whiner. She was absolutely pitiless. But I could tell she really loved the students. I asked her about her teaching philosophy. She said, "I'm cruel but fair. And I don't take any shit from the little fuckers."

She was a very dedicated teacher. I remember this problem with a bat I had in one of my classes. And I remember her reaction.

I was teaching away, amusing the students with some anecdote. I always use anecdotes from real life to force the students to relax. I find if I use things from my own life then I become more human to them. Some days, though, it takes a lot of anecdotes. So there I was, being anecdotal. But, of course, I was still saying things relevant to the whole "directing" experience, while at the same time trying to entertain. Then we hear this little whimpering sound. And one of the students suddenly jumps up and points to the corner. And pretty soon all of the students are pointing and we're all sort of staring. I think it's a dying mouse, of course. And then I finally wend my way to the corner. And sure enough, it's not a mouse whimpering there—it's a bat. I can't believe it. And the students, all of a sudden, are on the side of the bat. It's unbelievable. They're going, "Don't kill it. Don't you kill it." And I'm thinking, "Kill it, are you out of your mind? I wouldn't go near it!" I mean, I think I can make a generalization here and say that most human beings find bats the among most terrifying animals in the world. Everybody except for university students, I guess. *They* sympathize. I will admit it was a baby bat, and that made the students feel sorry for it. But to me, the idea that the bat (baby or not, sick or not) could at any moment open its wings and start zooming around the room absolutely terrified me. I'm sure that bats are the nicest animals in the world. (Later I met a cab driver who turned out to be a bat expert. He told me that bats *are* the nicest animals in the world and they would never hurt anyone.) So I'm running around—completely revealing that I'm a hysterical faggot teacher—terrified of the bat. The students found this very funny. I'm sure their other teachers would act very calm and responsible and say, "Excuse me, I'll just call the Humane Society. I'll be right back." But me, I screamed, "AHHH! Don't move! I'll run downstairs and get the bat person to come and take this fucking bat away. Good-bye." And they're yelling, "Don't let him kill it, don't let him kill it!" I could have cared less what the bat guy would do to it. I just wanted someone to take it away. Anybody. Meanwhile, I suggested one of the brave students cover the bat with a box and put some weight on it. They were still on about it. "We don't want to hurt him." Jeez.

Anyway, the bat guy from the Humane Society came and took the bat away. And everything did calm down. The next day, I told Pat about the whole bat thing and she was very funny about it. I told her about how desperate I was to get rid of the creature, and how I acted like such a fag. She found that very funny. And then I told her how concerned the students were that the bat was going to be harmed. She didn't have much sympathy for the thing. She said, "You know why that bat was in your class-room, don't you?" I told her I thought that the classroom was right near the old school belfry where bats might hang out. And she said, "Yeah, I know. But the thing is, that bat wouldn't have been lying on it's back whimpering if it wasn't sick." I told her I thought it had gotten lost. "Bats don't get lost," she said. I told her I figured the bat guy would fix up the baby bat. "Oh, no," she said, "if the bat is in such bad condition that it's lying on it's back and it can't fly, then they're going to kill it." "You're not serious!" I said. "Sure," she said. "It's going to bat heaven." "Oh, no," I said. "If the students found out they would be so upset." "That should be their next lesson," she said. "Good morn-ing, kids. The bat is dead. That's your first lesson of the day."

I didn't have the heart to tell them.

Bat or no bat, my life was quite ideal. What with the teach-ing, and the money, and the little gingerbread house, and my new friends, and my new lover. I think people sort of knew Matthew and I were lovers. But they didn't make a big thing out of it. As I said, Matthew never took me out in public. I couldn't help repeating intelligent things Matthew had said, though. So, I'm sure a lot of people knew. But as I said, it was a very waspy college. And even if people did resent it, they wouldn't have opened their mouths.

And so then the only fly in the ointment—the thing that really started the trouble—was that Matthew and I started to fall out of love.

I don't know exactly when it happened. It was sort of towards the end of the spring term. I think it was a combination of the students starting to wear shorts and Matthew and I being together for almost six months. That's a long time for me.

Gradually, I began to realize that I was not Matthew's ideal guy. I mean, there were signs. Early on, he told me that I was his "lawyer." I asked him what he meant by that, and he said it meant that I was his "sensible choice." "But I'm not a lawyer,"I said. "Yes, but you're not my usual type. You're not a boy, you don't have a drinking problem. You're an intelligent, functioning adult." Yes, I was. But that description didn't make me sound very attractive. "You know what I mean," he said, "you're a new thing for me, and I'm, well, I'm trying something new." This made me very insecure. I didn't think I liked the idea of being someone's "new" approach to life. I'd rather be someone's "old" approach, one they're more relaxed with. Also, I've never been a big fan of sensible choices in love. Myself, I've dated some guys who I figured would be perfect for me (they're smart, they're older, they're together) only to find that I don't want to lick their bums. To tell you the truth, bumlicking has always been my benchmark. If I don't want to lick their bum then I don't really love them. Now it's true I never wanted to lick Matthew's bum, but I figured…well, I figured he was so beautiful and smart it didn't matter.

But it did. It mattered that I wasn't his wayward drunken youth. But I think what mattered most of all was when Matthew realized that I was not his perfect "student." The longer we dated, the more honest I became with him. And gradually I stopped. At first, I would get drunk and say, "Yes, Matthew" when he lectured me. Later I stopped getting drunk just so I could be sober enough to look him straight in his brilliant blue eyes and say, "No Matthew. I think you're wrong. We disagree." He hated that. He just hated that so much. I was, ultimately, supposed to agree with him. But of course, Matthew was so charming that the discussion would never actually get nasty. And he tried very hard not to indicate that he was frustrated with me. Which he was. I began to realize that Matthew needed someone who, in effect, would always be his student. That meant someone who was either a little bit less intelligent or successful than he was, or just someone who would always be young. An eternal boy, the Peter Pan type. Finally, my resistance started to get me into trouble.

One night, I was blathering on about how much I liked teaching, because I really did. I was saying what a challenge it was to engage the students and how proud I was when I could. And then I talked about my techniques for keeping their interest. I blithely mentioned the fact that I do a little "self-revelation" in class. I mentioned that this one kid, for instance, had directed this play about a crazy woman.

You see, I was trying to make them understand how to direct actors who had to play "crazies." It's just so tempting for any actor to make "crazy" cute, or not—scary, or just plain wacky. I wanted them to know that there are some people in the world who simply communicate in ways that differ from normal logical conversation, for instance. And so I had decided to tell the class this great anecdote about a woman I had known who was really crazy.

Emma was a writer and I had been in one of her crazy plays. Her stuff was sort of written in another language. An example?

"I me we went out the limb the morbid limb which cracked when the eye pierced with pain and the night and you and the dark and love."

Now that's corny, but you get the idea. It seems, at first, to be stream-of-consciousness drivel. But then you realize that it's actually full of meaning. I think that's what separates good stream-of-consciousness writing from bad. That is, it has to make sense on some subliminal level: It should touch some Jungian archetypal chord. Anyway, Emma wrote good stream-of-consciousness stuff. And once I starred in this one play she wrote about a man who molests a woman. At the time, it was a big hit. I should have seen the writing on the wall, though. Emma saw *me* as a molester. I think that's why she cast me in the part, actually. I think she saw all men as molesters. And she had a hysterical Puritan background, filled with guilt and recrimination. She was from a family of New England ministers. It sort of accounted for the messianic tone of her prose. Also, she had a tendency to do a lot of prescription drugs. In fact, she had worked as a hooker now and then. So Emma would go through some periods that were crazier than others. When she was not so crazy, she'd speak in odd but basically understandable English. At those times she produced plays and performed poetry. But when she was going through a bad spell, she'd take drugs and hook. And speak in impenetrable code. Anyway, during one of her good spells, she married this guy who I found very attractive. And they were very liberal and stuff. And one night they asked me to have sex with them, and I said, "Okay." I mean, why not? Emma was kind of strange-looking, but he was hot and I figured (because he was so tall and lean) that he'd have a huge dick. And he did. It turned out to be less a threesome than me sucking this guy's cock. And sort of "helping" him fuck her. I didn't really want to fuck her. But it worked out okay. Later, they had a kid. Then her husband turned out to be gay. Now all this sort of freaked Emma out. Anyway, after their breakup the husband took the kid and had a sex change. And he sort of became the kid's mother. (I have such interesting friends!) All I could think of when I saw the guy in his new sex change drag was how much the world would miss his big dick. But Emma took it harder, of course. She got really weird and started to take drugs and hook again.

First she got mad at me, though. I was supposed to read some of her poems at a reading. Beforehand, in the lobby, she started yelling at me about my being a homosexual. She said dirty homosexuals were molesters of women. (What a thing for a registered homosexual to be accused of. You can lose your gaycard for just desiring women sexually. Never mind molesting them!) Then, a long time after that, we had an even more spaced-out encounter.

It was about ten years after I met her, and about seven years after I had sex with her and her husband. I had sort of forgotten about Emma, actually. I was walking home on a bright summer day and who should I meet walking up my street but Emma. She was looking very lousy, all dressed up like a hooker. She was obviously stoned. And then she came on to me. It was totally shocking. She wanted me to have sex with her. (She asked me in sort of a drugged, stream-of-consciousness way. But I knew what she was talking about.) Now after all I had been through with Emma, this was really weird. And it wasn't just a come-on, it was a business deal. She wanted money. And she had her hands all over me. I tried to make her realize that this was crazy. It's like, "Emma, this is Jack. Remember, I was in your play? I had sex with you and your husband for free? And I'm a homosexual? Remember?" She finally left me alone, but the whole thing was really sad and upsetting.

Well, I told this anecdote to my class. I will admit that I left out the part about sleeping with Emma and her husband. And I left out the part about her husband having a sex change. I basically just told them all about her stream-of-consciousness way of writing and talking. And I told them about meeting her when she was stoned. And how she tried to pick me up when she was a hooker.

In my little joyous, slightly drunk, monologue with Matthew, I made the mistake of telling him that I had told the students about Emma. He got very upset.

"But you musn't," he said.

"Why not?"

"Well, because you are breaking a sacred trust."

"Did I make a trust not to tell them about myself? Is that what you're saying?" As you could see, I was pretty far from my acquiescence at this point.

"Your personal life must always be a mystery to them."

"I didn't tell them I helped Emma's preoperative, transgendered husband fuck her," I said, in my defence.

"All I have to say is, thank God. Thank God."

"I don't understand, Matthew. What's the big deal?"

"The sacred trust is this: *We* are always a mystery to them. They want to know about our lives, of course they do, because they adore us, in that distant way. But in order for us to retain a kind of authority—not discipline really, this relates to knowledge—we must keep certain things a mystery."

"I really don't get it."

"You are not friends with them. The students are not your friends. They are your students. It's something very different."

"I think it's just a matter of style," I said, trying to diffuse the argument. "It's great that you like to maintain this distance, and it suits you. Matthew, you're handsomer than I am, you're older than I am. You're very charming."

"You're charming."

"Thank you, but my charm is based on confession. I love to confess." (I couldn't believe this—two old fags outcharming each other with charm accusations!)

"No, you musn't confess to your students. That's for the chapel."

I couldn't believe he said "the chapel." This man was not at all religious, as far as I could tell at the time. (Though I learned later that he did have a detailed knowledge of Butler's *Lives of The Saints*.) We left the argument there, and we got drunker and then went to bed and didn't have sex.

But we both knew that this had revealed a major difference between us. I felt very strongly about what I was doing. And I didn't think it was wrong. In my view, if students were going to learn, then part of their learning was going to be about me. After all, I was a human being standing in front of them. To ignore my humanity and just spout ideas would be such a waste.

Once I had a bad experience with a therapist that was analagous. He ignored both my humanity and his. It was very upsetting. He was this uptight, little, middle-class, gay therapist. In therapy, I had been very frank about liking younger men. I remember asking him once if that was "sick." And I remember him fingering a pen or something, and saying, very unemotionally, "Well, those kind of attractions are usually something that therapy cannot change." In other words, he agreed that my attraction for younger men was some kind of trick that God had played on me. And that I would be like that for the duration of my life. But that ended his elaboration on the subject. Note: he was the homely, bookish, chunky type. You couldn't imagine him having a sex life. Even though I know that some guys do go for homely middle-class guys like him.

Anyway, I stopped seeing him because he was doing nothing for me, really. And then about three months later I caught him leaving a local gay bar. Well! He was minus his spectacles and wearing an open-collar shirt (not a suit). And he didn't look chunky at all. And he was squiring this gorgeous blonde boy who was young enough to be his son. And they were not having a meeting. They were having drinks.

And I was so angry and jealous. But mostly angry. I thought, why didn't he tell me? He obviously has absolutely the same sexual tastes as me! And if only he had opened up about his sexual tastes in therapy instead of leaning back and stroking his pen and saying, "Well, those kinds of attractions are usually something that therapy cannot change." Maybe then we could have made a little progress! How different our therapy would have been if he had broken the stupid patient-client wall and said, "You're right. There nothing better than licking some fine young ass. But hey, I'd recommend a hepatitis shot!"

Now of course, I wasn't thinking of having conversations like that with my students. But I was honestly thinking that revealing myself—my personal feelings and experiences—was a valuable thing and part of learning. And I was beginning to think that hiding stuff from the students was a kind of crime.

If my authority (Matthew had used the word authority instead of discipline—what the fuck did he mean by that?) was based on hiding stuff from the students, what kind of authority was it? Shouldn't my authority be based on the pride I have in my own honesty? And on showing myself to them, warts and all?

Looking back on it now, I think Matthew was smart enough to know where this kind of thinking might lead. First, I think he recognized that I was more "out" than he was. I mean, Matthew was "out," I guess, in a way. But Frank was his beard. He would take Frank, the school administrator, with him to public functions. And in this way, he could sort of appease those politically correct fags who wanted him to be "out" about his homosexuality. He said to me once, "I never take a woman to these functions. I always take Frank. It's always myself and another man, in a tux, and, you know, people can come to their own conclusions. That's fine." And that was supposed to be so liberated of him. But he didn't take any of his Black boyfriends, did he? I mean, it's one thing to take a nice, respectable guy who's not your lover to a public function. It's something else to bring someone who you're obviously hot for. Someone who might play footsie with you under the table. So this was all part of the difference between our styles, between the old Brit and me. Matthew didn't like to tell all, he'd just sort of elegantly indicate. My problem with that was (and still is) precisely this: basically, I think the board at St. Stephen's, the trustees, and all the boring powerful people, could conveniently forget Matthew was a homosexual. And that was a kind of closeting. So Matthew wasn't about to talk about his personal life in class.

And I also think Matthew knew my confessions, my efforts to be "real" with the students, could perhaps lead to more dangerous things. He probably sensed I was "the man of the slow burn." When I learn, I learn slowly. But it stays learned. And I was just starting to discover that the students needed to know about me. And that they needed me to be honest. How many other adults were honest with them? To me, it was a sign of respect not to treat them like children. But once you start telling the truth and revealing, it can become addictive. You just can't stop.

So even though we got drunk and listened to some new Philip Glass afterwards, we knew there had been a rift after the big "Emma anecdote" argument. And I realized a very important fact about these May-December/teacher-student relationships. If they're going to continue, the student can never graduate. If the student/lover does graduate, it can be very sad. And that's what it became for us. A Mr. Chips sort of thing.

I will admit that I was sexually frustrated. We weren't having that much sex in the end. And the boys around campus were wearing shorts. There's something about teenagers in shorts. Then these boys would get on bikes. And the muscles in their legs would start working and I was a goner. I realized as much as I loved Matthew, my teacher and lover, I had to lick some boy-ass, basically, as soon as possible.

So I started taking off nights and going to the city. It was no big deal for Matthew, because we didn't spend every night together. But gradually, I think he began to realize I was leaving Stony Bay now and then. And we had such an intellectual friendship, and we had so much in common (even our attraction for young men), that I felt myself wanting to talk to Matthew about the boys I fucked in town. And I knew this would not be possible.

I also knew it would not be possible for me to continue teaching in Stony Bay and living there at the same time. I was beginning to miss the gay ghetto. And I knew this was going to be an issue. All of a sudden, I realized my job was in danger. What would happen to my job if I broke up with the dean and moved out of Stony Bay? And it was a job, that, unfortunately, I was starting to like.

I weighed the two things: telling Matthew that I wanted to break up with him, and telling him that I wanted to move out of Stony Bay. And I decided that telling him I wanted to move out of Stony Bay would ultimately be easier. And, in a way, more honest. I could imagine, actually, continuing a sort of part-time relationship with Matthew. And then commuting from the city to teach. This actually seemed like the ideal thing to do. Maintain a sexual friendship with Matthew and commute.

But it wasn't to be.

In fact, I really miscalculated that one. I can't believe how I underestimated Matthew's reaction. I had no idea he was so sensitive about living in Stony Bay. It was as if I was attacking his whole way of life. But my frustration with St. Stephen's and Matthew became very intense (what with staring at boys' knees). I knew that I had to live in the city again and get laid regularly.

I picked a springlike night in April to tell him about my commuting plans. I'll always remember that it was April 17. I noticed later that April 17 was St. Stephen's Day on the Saints' Calendar.

We were sitting around in Matthew's kitchen, having the usual evening wine and toke. I decided to spring the idea of moving to town for the summer semester. I just wanted to see how he would take it; I wasn't even thinking about breaking up at this point. I thought: this is natural. The relationship is running its course. I need some independence.

Well, he practically burst a blood vessel.

"You what?" he said.

"I was thinking it might be better for me to live in the city and commute."

"Are you out of your mind?"

How do you answer a question like that? "No, I don't think so."

"Do you realize what this is saying to me, to us at St. Stephen's?"

"It's saying I miss the city. I miss the opera. I miss the gay bars. I miss the hustle and bustle."

"I see. So you don't find St. Stephen's stimulating enough for you?"

"I didn't say that."

"That's what you seem to be saying."

"I just get bored very easily. I'm not a small-town guy. I told you about how frustrating it was for me, growing up in a small town."

"This is not just a small town. This is an intellectual epicentre. It has a heartbeat. This is the place where ideas start. I didn't think I'd ever have to say this to you, but it's quite a privilege for you to be here."

"I know that, Matthew, and I'm very grateful, I'll always be grateful."

"Then why are you leaving?"

"I'm not leaving. I just want to commute."

"How can you commute? You'll be too tired to teach."

"I only teach two days a week. The drive is an hour and a half. I can stay over. I can stay over with you, if you want me to."

"I don't think you understand." He turned away from me. I couldn't believe he was getting so emotional. "I'm very happy here. I've created this place for people like you to be stimulated and intellectually aroused. If you don't find it stimulating, what do you think it says about me?"

"I didn't say I didn't find it stimulating."

"That's what your actions are saying. Leave me alone. I don't want to talk about it anymore. Go. If you want to go, then go. Leave me. Leave St. Stephen's. It's quite all right with me if that's the way you feel. I'm not going to stop you."

Jesus. This was serious. I couldn't believe it. I'd never seen Matthew so emotional.

"But, Matthew—"

"Leave me alone."

Oh my God. He was so hurt. I didn't mean to hurt him. On my way out, I could see that something had been truly broken, ended. I had hurt him much more badly than I could imagine. And here I was thinking this would be a tactful way to ease up on our relationship. I mean, hadn't he noticed that we were having a lot less sex? He knew what a sexual person I was. Maybe it was fine for him, hugging three nights a week and then maybe having sex on the fourth. It was certainly not enough for me. And obviously we were disagreeing about ideas more than we ever did. In fundamental ways.

And then I saw that this whole thing, this whole teaching job, had been a gift from Matthew. It was a very special gift, and I was being very callous and selfish rejecting it. He *was* St. Stephen's, it was his life. Teaching was his life. And teaching was supposed to become my life too. And I was supposed to become the kind of teacher Matthew was, maintaining a distance from the students. Had Matthew mentioned my political activities once since I had arrived? No, he was trying to mold me, shape me into being a great, traditional-style teacher like him. Only I wasn't him, I was *me.*

And I'm a horny confessor, not an aloof, charming Brit. But I really had no idea that being different from him would hurt him so much. Because that's what the real problem was. He had taught me so much about Edwardian children and music and teaching itself. But that wasn't enough for me. I needed different kinds of knowledge—sexual knowledge, street knowledge. The kind of stuff a city and promiscuity would offer. Why couldn't he just accept that? Did it threaten him? Why couldn't people just be different? Why couldn't this student graduate?

I walked alone that night beside this particularly lonely boat-house near this mansion. Sometimes I liked to go out walking like that in Stony Bay. Feeling the "nature." Nature is good for making you feel the insignificance of your life and ideas, and for putting things in perspective. I walked around feeling very alone. Feeling that Matthew was the most handsome, intelligent man I had ever met. I remember thinking, well, that's it for me and older men. I mean, basically Matthew was the most fascinating, compelling, older man alive. And I didn't want him. I would have to be a boybumlicker forever.

It was a very sad time for me. I know you might think, "Oh great, the guy gets his jollies torturing older men and taking advantage of them." No. That was Alistair. That wasn't me. It's true. I know now that I am a boy lover. They've got to be boyish or boylike, or I just can't keep up the romance. But I honestly didn't know that until I met Matthew. I thought maybe I could change my sexual and romantic tastes, because I had met someone special. Like that therapist had said, "Those kinds of attractions are usually something that therapy cannot change." (And, he should also have said, "And something that can get you into trouble.") My problem is that I really need intellectual stimulation. And it's nice to get it from a lover, you know? But my lovers tend to have a very specific hair distribution, which disappears usually around age twenty-nine, the year when wisdom begins to descend (from wherever wisdom descends).

Of course, I expected to be fired. The term was over and the students were acting very strangely. They were getting quite emotional with me: I had a feeling they loved me. This made my impending professional doom seem more ironic. I remember the last day of my classes. David Lovejoy made this little speech about how much he enjoyed the class. He was very embarassed. It was very sexy. I began to realize that I was their only "out" teacher. I was probably the only homosexual they had seen besides the campy extremes they saw on TV (or the perfect middle-class extremes they saw dying of AIDS in movies). There was one girl I had in my class that term who actually changed in front of my eyes. She entered a sullen Biology major, who had very little interest in theatre. She had a chip on her shoulder and she wasn't very attractive. But partway through the course she started warming up to me. It seemed like my honesty was really appealing to her. She loved the anecdotes and started to change. She cut her hair and dyed it and started wearing funky clothes. I could tell it was me who was changing her, because at first she asked really challenging questions tinged with a provocative tone. A tone calculated to elicit bullshit. But I wouldn't give her bullshit answers. I'd even say "I really don't know" when I didn't. My honesty just made her bloom. By the end of the class, she was working really well. And she looked like a million bucks. She said she didn't know if she wanted to be a director. But she wanted to get out of Biology. (Half of these kids were just taking business or science courses because their parents wanted them to. A lot of them had double majors, one boring and one great. They'd say,

"I'm majoring in Business and Sexual Diversity." And guess who's encouraging them to take the business stuff? Mom and Dad, of course.) So I changed a life. At least it seemed to me I did.

At the end of term, another girl (she was sort of an oddball) asked me all these cute questions. All of a sudden she had to know about my personal life. "Where do you live? Do you have a cat? What do you do when you're not at school?" I didn't say "I fuck The Dapper Dean." But that's mainly because I wasn't fucking him very much anymore. I was pretty honest with her, though. And I saw how important it was for them to know about us. About us teachers as people.

And I felt more certain about my disagreement with Matthew, and I was very sad.

Maybe I would always have to date guys who weren't as smart as me. That way I would never have to disagree with them. (What's to disagree? You can't argue with a window washer about Barthes. So at least you know that you get along with each other in one area—semiology.)

Through all of these student goodbyes, I waited for my pink slip. But it didn't come. It was two weeks after the last day of class. It was two weeks until the summer semester would start. We were into the end of May, and I was supposed to teach two courses in acting (a beginners and an advanced) and no one had asked for my resignation. What was going on?

I talked to Lyle about it, and he was very philosophical. "Well, you're not the protégé anymore. You're not the blessed son. I guess it's back to Alistair for Matthew." This kind of irritated me. Lyle had this incredibly cynical way of talking about men. He totally dismissed romance. Perhaps the reason was in his past. He had been the "kept boy" of a serious British intellectual— someone very much like Matthew. The guy had committed suicide when Lyle was barely twenty-three. Since the suicide, Lyle talked like one of those people who never cared whether or not he fell in love. (I learned all about Lyle's past from Pat. Lyle never would have admitted it.) I decided to be very honest about love with Lyle. "I was in love with Matthew." "I believe you," he said. And he looked at me, very drunk. I actually thought his eyes were tearing up. "Sure you loved him. You must have. Since he's not at all your physical type." "So what will happen to me?" I asked, suddenly selfish, pouting. "Nothing," he said. "Nothing?" "Absolutely nothing. What were the last words Matthew said to you? What were they?" I answered. "Leave me alone." "We're talking British reserve here. I know Brit reserve." I thought of his boyfriend who committed suicide. "And that is the extent of the emotional admission you're going to get from him, buddy." "Do you think he'll fire me?" "I don't think he'll do anything. He'll do absolutely nothing. Just wait and see."

I thought of the incredible wellspring of emotion that could be waiting to burst inside Matthew. I thought about him calling me his "lawyer," his big try at a respectable relationship. Could it be possible Matthew was deeply injured by our breakup? Could the "sensible choice" be some sort of a final choice for him? A last chance before abandoning romance?

I decided to ask Pat about my academic future. I had a lunch with her and we gossiped and talked. She told me the students loved me. She said I should watch it because I obviously wasn't being mean enough to them. "Oh, they shouldn't love you too much," she said. And I thought, is that because you might start loving them back? And then I thought that was a silly thing to even consider. Pat wasn't like me—she wasn't attracted to her students. Pat was so sensible. We were having lunch at her little cottage. (St. Stephen's supplied cottages for the tenured professors as well as the guest professors like me.) And her Siamese cats were playing on the couch in the living room, next to her sunny dining room table, which was cluttered with books. She was awfully attached to those cats. They were

called Poomi and Syri and they had that cranky mystical tempera-
ment that so typify Siamese. As we talked, they scurried around
the room, taking different poses. All the while, they seemed to
be connected in some strange cat world, hearing cat music,
secretly dancing in synchronization. Pat loved her cats a lot.
She even talked to them. Was that projection? Was that because
she was a little afraid of how much she loved her students?
And is that why she pretended to hate them?

These teachers were starting to scare me. Pat told me not to
be scared. Though she did say something that freaked me out.
"Don't worry, you won't be fired." (Keep in mind I hadn't told
her about my teaching style. I hadn't told her anything about
my tendency to be ultra-honest with the students.) "Matthew
may have been in love with you, but he's not stupid. You know,
as an actor and an 'out' gay man, you lend a sort of cachet to
this little college. It would not be practical for Matthew to fire
you. And even if he is lovesick or hurt or whatever, that wouldn't
stop him from being practical. You don't become as successful
and secure in the academic world as Matthew has by making
rash decisions. I've heard no rumours about you being fired.
I'm sure you've been asked back. Poomi. What do you want?
What does little Poomi want? Is Syri monopolizing all the attention? Yes, Poomi wants some. My little Poomi. Come here.
That's it, my little boy. Doesn't that feel better, doesn't that feel
much better?" We ended up talking about her cats quite a lot.
Of course, why would she worry? She had tenure.

But Pat was right, and so was Lyle. Nothing happened. And
nothing happening was, in a bewitching way, scarier. In fact, I
began to anticipate meeting Matthew by accident—let's say, in
the toilet—and having it out with him. I wanted him to scream
at me, "You ripped out my heart!" or something. But somehow
we managed not to see each other. I heard he'd taken a two-
week vacation back in town outside London.

And then, of course, something did happen. It was very unsettling, and very "unMatthewlike." At least that's what everyone told me later.

It was the night before the first week of summer classes, and
it was also Matthew's birthday. Apparently it was the tradition at
St. Stephen's to have an annual party. And the weather was fine,
and humid, and a little foggy. The party was in this old house
that was uninhabited but lushly furnished. It had been a million-
aire's house, then a student residence. But at the time, no one
lived there.

The place was huge and a little scary—lots of faded, slightly
crumbling elegance. There were vast windows with long, billow-
ing, sheer curtains, and there were candles on the tables. I kept
thinking that one of the curtains was going to catch fire. And
that would be the end of St. Stephen's. Everyone was there. I
had been a little afraid of going. I knew that Matthew would be
back from his trip. But then I thought, better now than never.
I'm obviously still an employee at St. Stephen's. I haven't been
fired. (I'd gotten the student evaluations, and all the students
liked me. Pat would say they liked me almost too much.) Frank
was there, and so were Pat, Lyle, and Alistair. There was also
a bunch of old farty professors who always seemed a little
gay to me. But apparently they weren't. Everyone had their little
cocktail glasses in their hands, and the old stereo was playing
some sort of jazz. It would have been very romantic, actually,
if everybody hadn't been so old and dusty. When I walked in,
no one spoke to me. I kind of felt like nobody knew how to
treat me. I found Lyle in a corner and I started to gossip with
him. But he was very drunk. We both talked about academics
and how they don't know how to party. Sure enough, I over-
heard some conversations and people were actually talking
shop—they were incomprehensible. I forced myself to say hello
to Frank and he said, "Hello, Jack." That's all he said. Then he

moved on. But the "Hello" was so perfectly political. (I know you think I'm paranoid.) No, it was. Frank betrayed nothing. The subtext was "Oh, you're still here. And you'll be here this term. Okay." Like it was a fact that he neither loved nor hated. A fact that he could do nothing about. I moved into another room and I saw Alistair chatting up Matthew. I quickly moved out of the room. Hmmm. Matthew had a nice tan. (Surprising for London, maybe he stopped off in the Bahamas.)

Oh, I thought, what a quick little mover and shaker that Alistair is. And I felt sad that Matthew was probably going to go to bed with Alistair after the party and just lie there with him and *not* make love. Because there was no chance of it. Because Alistair would torture him.

Pat waved to me from another room so I went in to talk to her. She started talking about her cats, of course. She was a little drunk. This was very charming, since I'd never seen her drunk before. It was an odd conversation. She seemed kinda far away. She said that she was going to have to take her cats to the cat psychiatrist because they were fighting over her. I don't remember what she said, not exactly, because she wasn't being clear. It was something about how they were getting into fights because she was petting one of them more than the other. She said she had taken them to the psychiatrist once already and he had recommended they be put in separate rooms for a while and then gradually brought back together. She had tried this to no avail.

At this point in the conversation, someone interrupted—a boring professor—and Pat seemed so involved with what he was saying that I suddenly felt completely ignored. It seemed like she wasn't into talking to me anymore. I mean, she was probably just very interested in what the old fart was saying. But it didn't make me feel very wanted.

Have you ever had that happen to you at a party? Have you ever been happily talking to someone and had someone else walk up and completely ignore you and start talking to the person you were talking to? And it wasn't like the boring farty professor had said, "Oh, hi Jack, excuse me, I just must steal Pat's ear on Brecht," or something else kitschily pedantic. No, he just marched up and started talking to her. Ignoring me completely. So all I could do was sort of saunter away. Don't you just hate that? Trying to walk away from a conversation where you've just been ignored and treated like garbage? So you just sort of slink off and swill your drink and try and act nonchalant? But you know you're wearing your rejection like too much cologne.

And I began to feel like I did when I was eighteen and refused to go to Vietnam.

Let me explain. When I was a teenager, I decided not to fight in the Vietnam War. I wrote my grandparents a letter about it (my small-town grandparents, the Fascist ones). I told them I was a conscientious objector. I thought I was being open, and honest, and brave by telling them. Well, that was a big mistake. They were very cruel to me. They were very angry, but like Matthew, they didn't show it openly. They were what I call "wasp" angry—which is much worse. They simply ignored me. Literally.

We went to visit my grandparents. My grandmother hugged my mother (who she didn't even like very much), and my sister, and my dad. But she didn't hug me. When I approached her, she turned away. That whole evening my grandparents sat in the same room with me. But because I refused to fight in Vietnam they pretended I wasn't there. They directed conversation past me. It was as if I had become invisible.

It was the last time I saw them alive.

And I began to feel that way about St. Stephen's. Maybe I wouldn't feel so good about continuing to teach here if I didn't exist. If nobody really wanted to talk to me. It almost seemed as if Matthew had sent out a message (a very subtle one), that said, "Don't talk to him. He's over." Like a telepathic memo. I know that's a very paranoid thing to think. But, of course, with all the tension of party-going, I had quite a few vodka martinis. There was mist out on the perfectly manicured green lawns. (Matthew was really into gardening and landscaping at St. Stephen's. One year, he even had some of the bushes cut into shapes like the bushes in *The Draftsman's Contract*. Did you see that movie? Matthew rented the video for me because he loved it so much. I felt like such an idiot. I hated it. I felt so dumb.) There was dew forming on the beech trees. The curtains were blowing in the warm, early, summer breeze. It was like one of those alien movies. They were all on the planet of St. Stephen, and they had frozen me out.

I felt very sad and then angry, like I get sometimes when I'm very drunk. And I wanted to quit. Maybe it had been all about Matthew. Not teaching. Maybe I had learned what I was meant to learn at St. Stephen's. That I really loved boys—no more older deans for me. I would never be a teacher. Without Matthew around, I would desire the boy students too much. I would have to quit. I staggered into an upstairs bedroom, where there was a huge gilt mirror and a fireplace. I glanced in the mirror. I did not look very attractive. So I did the "thin face" that I do (which didn't help) and wandered over to a window. Suddenly, the door of the room blew shut. And Matthew was standing behind the door. It seemed very dreamlike. I don't remember too many details, just a few of the things Matthew said. He staggered over. (I was drunk, but he was much drunker than me and probably stoned, too.) And he sort of wavered by the window. I remember wanting to hold him, fearing he might fall out, down, on to the perfectly manicured lawn. Suddenly, he spoke, in a very soft voice. "Don't leave me," he said, "please...don't leave me."

Such a blatant revelation of emotion was absolutely heartbreaking and totally uncharacteristic. After nearly a month of silence? I couldn't handle it. I wanted to run out of the room. Somewhere in the distance Blossom Dearie was singing about Manhattan. It seemed so far away. We were here, in the country, in a place I'd never been. At one point, I remember, he staggered, and I thought he was going to fall again. And then he held up his hand to the window, so that some of the light coming from the moon seemed to penetrate it. You could see his old man's veins. They were bluish. "Look." And he laughed in that light, helpless way he had of laughing after sex. Now I realized it was not connected with sex, really, it was just his terribly drunken laugh. "Look, you can see through my hand." He laughed again. "It's the austerity of our monastic days." He laughed and said the word again. "Monastic." Then and his head bobbed down on his chest as if he were going to become unconscious. Then he flung his head back and he looked young again. There was a sparkling blue in his eyes, and I realized they were wet with tears. A lock of straight hair fell over one eye in an amazingly boyish way. "Denial. It's about denial, don't you understand? Don't you think I want them? Don't you think I want them more than you do?" He was very angry suddenly and it frightened me. I couldn't stand it anymore. I walked towards the door. Before I reached it, I heard him say again, "Please, don't leave me." I opened the door and I heard him stumble, and I heard a little helpless, drunken laughter.

Of course I left the party after that. After all, this was what I came for, wasn't it? I was tired of being treated like a non-person. I was tired of getting no reaction. Now I had my reaction. But what did it all mean? Monasticism? Denial? Obviously, Matthew took this whole teaching thing a lot more seriously than I did. Maybe I was messing with something dangerous.

I went right home after that. It was very unnerving. I really was beginning to think that I was getting involved with something scary.

The next day, under the pretense of having a post-party gossip breakfast with Lyle, I pumped him for information about Matthew and St. Stephen's. I tried to be subtle. I thought Lyle could put it all in perspective. Then maybe I wouldn't feel like the town was filled with aliens. Maybe Lyle would talk me into staying.

But what Lyle told me was sort of unsettling. I told him the monastic stuff. The stuff about Matthew holding his hand up to the light and saying that you could see through it. This all seemed logical to Lyle. "He sees himself as a monk. He's taken orders. He's given up his life to educate the young."

"Do you really think he takes it that seriously?" I asked.

"Absolutely. You know, this place wasn't called St. Stephen's before you got here."

"No?"

"It was called Kensington College. After a very rich lady who contributed half her life savings to it. No, Matthew paid some-one off and renamed it. He renamed it because St. Stephen was the founder of the Cistercian Order. He basically thinks of this place as a monastery. He has lots of theories about it. About giving up things. I've never really understood them."

"Has he talked about giving up sex?"

"No, he's never talked about that. He talks about asceticism. In some of his lectures about teaching, he talks about denial. He seems sort of vague about what you deny. Apparently, you can deny anything. I didn't pay much attention. I thought it was all just sort of a big publicity campaign for the college. An at-tempt to make it seem like a special sort of place."

All this made me want to find out more about St. Stephen. I went to the library right after breakfast, which is something I hadn't done since high school. My first summer semester class was the next day. So if I was going to make a decision about staying, I'd have to decide soon.

The library I went to wasn't the ordinary one. It was the

Religious Studies library for Divinity students and it was very extensive. I didn't think there were so many Religious Studies majors at St. Stephen's, but I guess I was wrong. The most amazing thing was that everyone in there was basically non-white. Not the staff, of course. I'm talking about the students (though I only saw about ten of them). As I mentioned, St. Stephen's was a very white university. So this was where the ten Asian and Black students hung out, eh? Count 'em, ten. How bizarre.

Immediately, I felt guilty about being there. I wasn't a Divinity student at all (far from it). I had basically defected from church as early on as was humanly possible. (Though I do remember having an epiphany once, in church. Just sitting there listening to the music, light streaming through the stained glass windows. I'm pretty musical, though. So I think it was the music.)

I wondered if everyone at the library knew I was a homo-sexual. And if they knew that I was doing research about my tragic, drunken, older ex-lover, who also happened to be their "Dapper Dean." The woman who helped me out was granny-like and efficient. She really had a handle on the computers, I thought. I figured her grandchildren must be really proud of her. I decided I'd just look under St. Stephen and see what the experts said. The best book seemed to be Butler's *Lives of Saints*. It had every saint listed, at least. And, of course, there were about ten St. Stephens. One was from Hungary, and one was a big martyr. (This sounded very much like the way Matthew was acting now, so I looked it up. It didn't seem very relevant.) And then I found a Stephen named Stephen Harding. Uh-oh (as Sherlock Holmes used to say, I think). A clue. Matthew Harding, Stephen Harding. It turns out that this particular St. Stephen was the founder of the Cistercian Order, the one Lyle mentioned. It was all starting to fit together.

I read on.

The part about the founding of the Cistercians was pretty

boring, filled with hardship and triumph. The usual Christian stuff. Then I came to something interesting:

"Their numbers diminished. A mysterious disease appeared amongst them which carried off one monk after another, until even Stephen's stout heart quailed before the prospect of the future, and he began to wonder if he were really doing the will of God. Certainly no one could have seen how dramatically the answer would come. At the monastery gates appeared one day a troop of thirty men, who announced to the astonished porter that they had come to crave admittance and they had as their leader and spokesman a young man whose name was Bernard. He had been moved to give up the world, but being of keen affections he had no mind to enter the way of perfection himself and leave his friends outside."

Now this was really too much. First of all, my middle name was Bernard (John Bernard Spratt). Could Matthew have picked me to come and teach because of my middle name? And secondly, there was just the whole gay nature of this story.

Hey, I know you're going to say that's stupid. You're going to say I read "gay" into everything. It's like when I told my mother that Cary Grant was gay. She was horrified, like, "Oh, no, not that! Why are you telling me that?" It's not as if I told her he was a serial killer in his spare time or something. Jeez. Sometimes I have this urge to really scare her. My mother just loves Gene Kelly. Someday, just out of spite, I'm going to come bouncing over to dinner, and then in the middle of the Welsh rarebit I'll lightly say, "Oh, did you know Gene Kelly was gay?" Like I was giving her the latest news on Bran Flakes or something. Then again, I don't want to give her a heart attack. (But you have to wonder: tight shirts, tight pants, not very American of him, was it?) Well, you might think it disgusting that I would read homosexuality into some old story about monks. But think about it.

It seems, to me, anyway, that a lot of those monks might

have been gay. It's practically been proven that when men hang out anywhere too long without women, well, it just happens. And also, this was a time (about 1064 or something) when priests were just beginning to be celibate. So this whole "anti-sex" thing was a new idea. Actually, I know a lot about this whole period because once I was in a play about Gilles deRais. He was the model for Bluebeard. I played Gilles deRais, of course. A wacky gay friend of mine wrote the part for me, hoping to capitalize on my gay reputation. It was a really good play. (Supposedly all the fags were going to run out to the theatre to see me, their hero, playing the biggest gay villain of all time. Well, you can forget it. First of all, fags won't go out of the house for anything except a blow job or the opera. For most fags, that's the ideal night, by the way. A blow job, and then the opera. Of course, they only talk about the opera part.) Anyway, you probably don't know this, but Bluebeard was really a gay guy. Yeah, he didn't kill his wives, he killed boys. They just cleaned up the stories in Grimm or whatever because it would have been just *too* grim to have a gay killer in medieval times.

Anyway, old Gilles deRais was quite a colourful character. All the mothers would come to his castle and say, "My boy has disappeared, and he was such a beautiful boy!" And old Gilles deRais would just twirl his beard and say, "Search me!" Apparently, he could get away with murder because nobles could pretty well take a shit at dinner and everyone would applaud. It was never proved that he killed anybody, but he was burned at the stake anyway. Probably for being a homosexual. Old Gilles used to say, "Your boys disappear because they grow up! They die!" Which was pretty true for the time. Lots of kids did disappear due to natural causes. So maybe he was innocent. But this play was all about the origin of Christianity and I learned a lot from it. I had to read this essay by Bertrand Russell called "Why I am Not a Christian." Did you know, for instance, that when

Christianity started they had to make all these rules that said things like "Nuns shouldn't fondle each other"? And, "Monks shouldn't masturbate during service"? This was because, at the time, the pagan religions were much more sexual. People actually associated religion with sex. Christianity changed all that.

So it seemed to me that it was a good bet that these monks might have been getting off together now and then (havin' a little ol' monk orgy). And just think of poor St. Stephen with all of his monks dying of some mysterious disease. (Gee, sounds like AIDS, huh?) And he's getting really lonely and tired of eating steamed potatoes. Then along comes Bernard, obviously a beautiful young guy. (I mean how else could he convince all these people to follow him if he wasn't good looking?) And Bernard just knocks at the door and says, "I am your student. Stephen, teach me how to be a great monk."

Now I tried reading this while thinking of Matthew reading it for the first time. I tried to think of him knowing all of this stuff, and how it must have been when he met me. My middle name is Bernard and I'm quite good-looking. (At least I must have looked boyish to Matthew, who was older) Maybe I was his new hope. I mean, that's the only explanation I could come up with to explain how emotional Matthew had gotten about everything between him and me. And all the stuff about being an ascetic? And his hands?

I also looked up some stuff about Bernard. He grew up to be St. Bernard. (Funny, huh? I wonder if they named the dog after him.) And this St. Bernard guy actually looked pretty interesting, too. Turns out he wrote some sermons about the Song of Songs. That sounded like it could be juicy. I made a note that I'd have to look up the Song of Songs later. Wasn't the Song of Songs the only sexy part of the Bible? The part the evangelists always conveniently forget to quote from? I figured this guy must be a majorly cool dude if he was writing about the Song of

Songs at a time when Christianity was just starting to get so re-
pressive. At this point the sweet old lady came and told me my
time was up. Not being a Divinity student or a Divinity professor meant that I had only half an hour to read about old St.
Bernard. I would have to come back later.

So now it all seemed pretty clear to me. Matthew saw himself as an ascetic sort of saint, and I was the young saint (in
training) who was supposed to carry on his work. It wasn't just
a love thing. No wonder he got upset. He probably saw me as
something like Matt Damon in *Good Will Hunting*. And he would
have been Robin Williams—like in my sex fantasy.

You know what disappointed me about *Good Will Hunting*?
Gus Van Sant directed it, and he's a gay director—a good one.
So why the hell didn't he bring out the sexual tension between
Robin Williams's and Matt Damon's characters? I mean, there
was obviously love between these two guys. But the producers
had to make them both so hysterically heterosexual. I mean,
each of them had to confirm that they were heterosexual, in
some way or other, every ten seconds or so. Just in case we
forgot. Just so we wouldn't for one moment think this was
a daddy/boy gay love affair.

I pity poor Minnie Driver, you know? Not only did Matt
Damon drop her right after the movie, and before the Acad-
emy awards, but her only purpose in the film was to keep reminding us that Matt Damon's character wasn't gay. Sometimes
Hollywood's so fucked. Matthew was the Robin Williams of
my life—the kind, older teacher character. And I had fallen
short of all his dreams for me. I sure would have liked to have
confirmed this with Matthew. But after our little encounter in
the old mansion I was afraid to talk to him. Though probably
he would have handled any encounter with his Brit politeness.
Politeness, of course, is ultimately more chilling than anger.
The big difference between Matthew and I was in the area of

how intimate a teacher should get with the students. Or, more specifically, in how much pleasure a teacher is going to get from the students emotionally. (At the time, I thought I just meant emotional pleasure. But this idea grew to include something physical later.)

I began to feel that teaching in the new semester without Matthew to guide me would be like embarking on a new journey. A new learning experience. It was going to be kinda scary. But let me say that I definitely didn't think it would lead to the "wildness" it did. In fact, I figured that I had all of my feelings for the students under control. I was getting fucked like crazy on my days in the city.

I was commuting. I had moved back to my little apartment in the centre of the gay part of town, and it was quite a welcome respite from St. Stephen's. Hey, don't let anyone tell you that promiscuous sex isn't totally fulfilling. Sometimes it definitely fulfills every goddamn need you have going. And you're not being honest if you say it doesn't. I know it's supposed to show how immature I am (and how unloving I am) that I like to fuck around. But I just don't happen to think so. I had this straight girlfriend once who said, "What about the emptiness afterward?" I didn't know how to tell her at the time, but my one-night stands were usually more like three-in-one-night stands. And I didn't feel empty afterwards. I never felt fucking empty, and you can quote me. And if I sound defensive, it's because I'm tired of uptight straight people telling me how "empty" I should feel. Hey, I feel a lot more "empty" after having bad sex with a boyfriend who I'm trying to pretend I love. Or a boyfriend who I love a lot and I'm trying desperately to have good sex with.

I felt a hundred times more "empty" on those nights when Matthew fell asleep drunk or stoned and we didn't have sex than I did on the nights when I was out in the city, fucking. The only time you feel empty after promiscuous sex is when you expect it to be something it isn't—emotionally fulfilling. Which is the mistake that a lot of young fags and straight people make. Looking for love in all the wrong places, you know? But if you don't set out looking for love, then when love does happen (when some cute boy is chowing down on you in some park or bath-house and he looks up at you, and you know he wants a date), you go, "Hey, love, come on in. Sounds like fun." But you don't go looking for it in the bushes.

I have had amazing encounters with people in bathhouses. And I still continue to do so. There's this one guy I've slept with a couple of times who is completely closeted and sweet. He looks like some sort of preppy boy. And when he's drunk and I meet him at the baths, he's kind of a one-man Comedy Central. He loves to imitate the guy with the rubbery face— you know, Jim Carrey. And he's totally into me because he likes my largeness. Actually, I'm not quite large enough for him. And when he sleeps with me at the baths, it's so sweet. He goes to sleep saying, "We have to do something together tomorrow, we have to have fun tomorrow, okay?" This is so incredibly touching. Of course, when the guy gets up in the morning (I usually don't sleep at the baths, except with this guy) it's all I can do to get him to have a coffee with me. (Forget the eggs!) He runs off. He has to get home to his house in the burbs where he lives with a couple of straight guys who don't know he comes down to the gay village. If you can believe it. The encounter is very sad and touching and I wouldn't miss it for the world.

Then there's the danger. Those guys who you think might just kill you or mess you up, or, yes, come in your ass without a condom. (Though I won't let anybody NEAR my ass without one.) Or even guys who call you faggot. No, really, you know Jilly, my crazy actress pal? She has gotten to the age where she doesn't have sex anymore. She says that sex goes with drinking.

And she stopped drinking. She is such a cool lady. I was talking to her one night just before going out to get laid. I told her I was looking for some dangerous excitement. "Sex," she said, "is only good when it's dangerous."

Jilly knew Edie Sedgwick. I know this sounds like a hellish digression, but she used to be married to this guy from a rock band and she used to hang out with Warhol and all his friends. (As you can probably tell, Jilly is a really wild character. An ex-alcoholic who is completely inspired and compassionate and she loves to hang out with fags. But she isn't a fag hag. No sir, Jilly is a gay man. There are women like that. They aren't sympathizing or condescending with fags. They don't get offended or hurt by your promiscuities like some fag hags do. They just happen to be gay men living in the bodies of women. Jilly's one of those.) She told me a lot about Edie Sedgwick and it just seems to epitomize the crazy dangerousness of the urban experience. And why I like to hang out there. She told me Edie was like totally unable to even make tea. She'd say, "Edie, would you like some tea?" And Edie would say, "Sure. I'll make it." And Jilly would say "Okay" really skeptically because she knew that Edie was missing the vital electrical connections in the brain that handle ordinary life. Apparently Edie would sort of move towards the cupboard and point at it and say, "Tea?" And Jilly would go over and take the tea out of the cupboard. Then Edie would say, "Do you have any cups?" And Jilly would say, "Yes." And well, you get the general idea. Edie was actually incapable of making a cup of tea. And though Jilly knew it was partly because Edie was so stoned, she also knew it was mainly because she had been so rich. Where Edie was brought up, it was the servants who made a cup of tea.

The point here is that you don't meet people like Edie on a farm. You don't meet them at St. Stephen's (unless you're really lucky, like I proved to be later, sort of). You meet them in some big city in a bar. Which is why all the evangelists stay out of the city. My friend Jilly and all her stories about Warhol sort of epitomized city life for me. We would meet for a drink sometimes before I'd go out to trick. She'd go, "Drink, drink, I want to see you drink." She was sort of drinking through me.

So I was happy with my commuting. The difficulty was, though, that I wasn't really unattracted to the students in my new class. And I could see that this was going to be a problem.

At first, I thought it was just because I wasn't in love with Matthew anymore. Except, in a way, I was still in love with him, of course—but I certainly couldn't fool myself that there was a big sexual attraction between us anymore. It was more about having someone to look up to and admire. It's really hard to find older men to admire if you're a fag. (I know that sounds horrible, but it's true. How many fags old enough to be my father were not brought up to be self-hating? Most fags that are my dad's age drink too much trying to forget they're gay. Sorry. But it's true, even if it's not their fault.) And (at least in the era when I grew up) real straight dads were trained to be cold and unfeeling. Nothing against my own dad, but we had absolutely nothing in common. He knew it and I knew it. And the things I showed an interest in (music, figure skating, and ballet for Chrissakes) were things that no decent red-blooded dad would dare to get excited about. I pity my father for having a kid like me; he was the "guy in the grey flannel suit." He was really very nice and loving underneath (if he ever did actually show emotion, which was rare). When my parents divorced, my mum criticized him a lot. (Understandably. Listen, I don't want to trash my parents. They are both very nice.) But various things (which my mother told me about) made it a bit difficult to love him sometimes. Actually, I'm going to stop talking about my father and mother now. It's too dangerous.

Let's just say that my real dad was distant. Not because he was a cruel guy, but because we were miles apart on every level.

So, of course, for me to find an older role model who was simply interested in stuff I was interested in was a great cause for rejoicing. I remember my first role model was Miss O'Brian. And you'll never guess what she used to do. She was a librarian. I remember she was an extremely tall, older woman with prominent breasts and spectacles on a rubber band. She used to stand up before every library class and read to us from *Oliver Twist* or something. I was in love with her. (I remember I told my mother I wanted to be a librarian when I grew up. She said, "That's nice, but I'm sure you'll grow up and find a more challenging occupation." Unfortunately I told Miss O'Brian my mother's advice because I was too young to know better. I think I hurt her feelings.) I worked every day at the library after school. And I read every biography of every human being that ever existed. I was addicted to biographies. When you think of it, they are the best thing around. They always have a great, automatic plot, and yet they're the truth. I never miss *Biography* on A&E. I was obsessed with Miss O'Brian because she was the first person I knew who could be as passionate about art as I was. But when I did get into "the arts" I got into theatre, where most of the people are, frankly, pretty stupid. So to quit theatre and then suddenly meet a handsome intellectual like Matthew, who was a man that I could, well, idolize—it was everything for me. And the idolization wasn't going to stop soon. (Even though I disagree with him on some topics to this day, I still remember him with affection. And I still wonder if some of his ideas—even the ones I hate—may be right.) Of course, at the time my idolization just made me want to rebel even more. I loved him so much that I just had to show my stuff, like any kid. Yeah, there will always be a little bit of Matthew in me. There will always be that image of him in the huge mansion, holding up his hand to the moonlight.

But Matthew was simply "done for" as a possible erotic object.

And I attributed my problems with the boys in my summer class to this.

What else do I attribute my newfound horniness for students to? Well, the fact that the boys in my summer class were cuter than the ones in my spring class, and, of course, they were wearing shorts.

The cuteness thing, I realized later, had a lot to do with the subject matter of the class. In my directing classes, I got the homely kids. Who else would take "directing"? I mean, let's face it, if you matched up pictures of all the great artists and writers in the world (as teenagers or adults) with pictures of ordinary people, I think the ordinary people would win the beauty contest. Actually, writers are usually the ugliest people in the world. I admit there are a few writers who always were hot. Have you ever seen pictures of Hemingway when he was a reporter for the *Toronto Telegram*? What a completely fuckable babe. (And the guy must have been a little queer. All those guns. And that prose. Very ejaculatory.) But then there's the young Tennessee Williams or the young Carson McCullers looking like they just crawled out from under a compost heap where someone was storing anemia, old warts, and spectacles. Okay, so Truman Capote was cute. A little too cute, actually. And F. Scott Fitzgerald was quite a babe. (It's a shame that Zelda went nuts, though.) And Kerouac was a doll until the booze got him. (The good-looking ones do have a tendency to die young.) But what about W. H. Auden and Lillian Hellman? (They just must have been related, don't you think?) And Joyce and T. S. Eliot and good old Oscar Wilde? Sometimes I think the price you have to pay for being a great writer is a good chin. That's what happens—when you're lining up for genius they say, "Sure, I give you a great imagination, instant alliteration and even good spelling. But what you get back is no chin."

Well, the boys in my directing classes were all chinless wonders. Except for the boy with the fortunate name of David Lovejoy. And he was such a closet case he scared me. But oh, boy, what about those perfectly ordinary old kids taking Beginners and Advanced Acting! I'm sorry, but these boys were hot. In fact, they were all so hot that I even noticed the girls! I had one girl who looked like she was part Fijian, part Swedish, and part Black. In other words, she was incredibly exotic. She had slightly slanted eyes, dark skin, and blonde hair. She was wildly beautiful with all the grace and poise of a young colt. (See how corny I get when I try and describe female beauty? Here's a good theory for why there's so much bad descriptive writing in the world: when you're closeted and you're pretending to get excited about the wrong gender, that's the result.)

Now the boys.

There were three boys in my classes who were unbearably gorgeous. Peter, Brock, and John James.

There were some other cute guys, too, but I won't mention them because they were minor in comparision to the glory of "The Three."

Number One: Peter. He was so lithe and handsome. Slender and small-hipped (for sure he'd have that lovely little treeline of hair going down from his belly button to his pubes) with big eyes and full lips. Just begging to suck on mine and then get fucked. Peter was a big, ideal student fantasy. I dreamed he'd lick me up and say, "Thank you, sir." He was an unconscionable flirt. Absolutely sexual, all the time. And straight, I think. But you know the kind of guy who is flirtatious with everyone (male or female) and so horny that you figure he'd fuck anything that moved (and some things that don't)? That was Peter. He toyed with me, cruelly. I remember one day I thought the best way to triumph over this attraction was simply to ignore it. And try and chat more equally with him. (Half the time it was just the fact that these boys were calling me "Sir." I figured if I could get them to stop calling me "Sir," I wouldn't be so turned on anymore. I don't know if you're aware of it, but in gay porn the word "Sir" is more of a turn-on than a big dick. The bottom always says "Yessir!" to the top. Porn stars have built whole careers on their ability to say "Sir" in the sexiest voice possible. So the first thing I had to do was get these boys to stop calling me "Sir." It just made me want to jack off.)

So, early on in the Advanced Acting course, Peter comes up to me and says, "Sir." I immediately go, "Call me Jack." And he smiled that winning smile of his—it leaves me weak in the knees even without the "Sir"—and then he asked me the question. (I can't remember what the stupid question was. It doesn't matter. He was just trying to torture me.) I thought I would try and be really relaxed with him, friendly. Maybe that would wipe out the sexual tension. Maybe all the sexual tension was about the age and class division. The fact that he was my "boy" student and I was the "man" teacher. Maybe if I evened things up it would be better. So I just casually said, "Nice necklace, Peter," because he had a little necklace. It was sitting ever so delicately, ever so gently on his neck, resting at the top of his hairless, slender chest. And it looked to me like it was a free-form modern sculpture image of—what? I wasn't sure. It looked like a Madonna and child. I thought it was a religious icon. I really did. So Peter goes "Thanks a lot, Jack." (He was being very sexy and awkward about using my real name. But after all, I had asked him to.) "My friend gave it to me. But the statistic refers to him, not me." And then he smiled and laughed. And so did I. Then I realized that his fucking necklace was not a Madonna and child. It said "Nine and a half." (Meaning nine and a half inches, of course!) So I got really red in the face and laughed like an idiot and said, "Oh, sorry, I didn't realize." This just made it worse, of course. And he looked at me quite pointedly. And I just wiggled away.

I felt so humiliated. I went and told Lyle about it that night at The President's Place. He was my best source of advice about students. I could ask him advice without having to worry about Matthew's "ascetic" censoriousness (not that Matthew was speaking to me anyway). I asked Lyle, "Was it just in my imagination? Did I imagine the whole thing? Or was this kid torturing me?" Lyle said, "Of course he was. They love torturing gay teachers. I used to know this one teacher at UConn who was an obvious fag and the boys there used to drive him crazy. They made some sort of a pact, and they would all sit in the front row of this old fag's lectures wearing shorts. Then they would spread their legs. It would drive him completely crazy. And some of them didn't wear underwear." I found this unbelievable to imagine from a usually homophobic student populace. But Lyle assured me it was true. A lot of these students may claim to be straight as hell, but it seems perfectly permissible to flirt with, and torture, their gay teachers.

Number Two: Brock. Brock gets the second vote because a) he had a porn-star name and b) he was brilliant. This was an unbeatable combination. I always think of Shakespeare's little obsession in the sonnets. (Those were written for a boy, by the way. Okay, maybe the last ones were written for some "Dark Lady." But she was Shakespeare's competition, not a love object. The first ones are definitely for a boy "pricked for women's pleasure" or whatever the line is. And there's more proof where that came from. I'm just too lazy to look it up.) Anyway, Shakespeare's big obsession is for the inside and the outside of the boy to match. For the boy to be both pretty and wise. Of course that's tough to find anywhere. And when Shakespeare figured he'd found the boy who matched inside and out, he got really happy and horny and wrote a whole passel of poetry. I think what was so alluring about Brock was that he matched inside and out. I mean, as far as I could tell. He could, of course, just have been sucking up to me. He could have been a hellraiser (in a bad way) outside of class, I don't know. But he was a perfect student inside mine. He always made contributions when I said, "Any questions?" (This is a godsend. As any teacher will tell you. Half the time, the students just sit there and look at you like you're invading valuable daydreaming time. I try and make fun of the situation. Sometimes I say, "Don't you all answer at once!" Which is not very funny—it just makes me feel more like Mrs. Krabapple on *The Simpsons*. Then I say, "Okay, if somebody doesn't say something, I'm going to have to pick someone, don't make me do that, it's so highschool.") But with Brock, it would never get to that point. He'd always have something to say, and that something was usually pretty smart. He worked hard. Brock was, without a doubt, my favourite fantasy youth. He was about six foot four with straight blond hair combed high off his face. He had startling blue eyes and a charming smile. But the key to Brock's attractiveness was his bigness. Big thighs, big arms (hair on them), and a naturally big chest. He was a big guy. The kind of guy that other guys always ask, "You play football?" He was my size, only younger and cuter and hairy all over, which is usually not a turn-on for me. But in Brock's case, I could forgive anything, imagining my tongue in that big furry butt. I also had the feeling that he'd learned old Mr. Lowenstien's lesson about the cows already. I just had this feeling that he knew how to throw a really slow fuck. Now normally, I don't get fucked. But I would make an exception with Brock, because he was so big and furry and...I won't go on. Oh yeah, one more thing about Brock. He made me so horny that I could barely talk to him. And he knew it. I'm absolutely sure that he knew I was gay (everybody did) and he tortured me about it. Whenever he asked me a question (and he often stayed after class to ask one), it was all I could do to control myself and not jump him.

104 — Sky Gilbert

Number Three: John James. There always has to be a comic one, a wacky one, a "Mr. Personality." That was John. Of course the fun started when I couldn't remember his name. Which, as I said, was rare for me with boy students. But with him, I could remember the two words, John and James. But I could never remember which of his names was first or last. (Do your kids a favour, heterosexual couples, don't give them two first names or two last ones like Whitney Sydney or Coleman Allen. It will drive people crazy, especially horny old teachers. I know the urge to be boring and safe is just too much for you straight white people sometimes. And I certainly understand. You wouldn't want your kid named Oleander Smith, or Alloysius Jones. But interchangeable names could lead to trouble later on.) So I immediately started having fun with this. I called him James sometimes and John other times. He would act "hurt." And this little routine went on and on. Then, of course, he proved tardy and, in fact, absent a lot of the time. So I'd say things like, "I thought you'd dropped the class John, or is it James?" And we just got into this ridiculous endless flirtation thing. He'd end up being very fake or perhaps real hurt. I think he was faking it (but it was still fun).

All this would be going on in front of the class. And frankly, it was because he had these beautiful muscles. He was another big one, but hairless. And he was tall. And he must have worked out at the gym all the time. He had one of those gigantic butts that made me want to bury my nose inside it. And he was very conscious of his huge, muscled body. He was always touching it. I sure wanted to, too. My endless flirting-over-lateness-and-absentness relationship with James/John made me think of the relationship I had with one of my teachers at university. I always arrived in class just on time. This old coot finally said to me, "Could you just arrive at class, in the future, a little bit before class is scheduled to start?" And I said, "No. I always arrive just on time. What's the problem?" "That's the problem, just on time," the prof said. "You're so close to being late every day that I'm worried you might actually be late. So could you come early every day?" I should have told him to take an enema. Looking back on it now, he must have had the hots for me to worry so much about my "lateness."

So now that I've finished fantasy raping and pillaging and licking and shoving my tongue up the butts of all my Acting students, you probably feel like putting down this book. I'll admit, so far, it hasn't exactly been Oprah-Pick-of-the-Week material. But it hasn't dealt with anything really repulsive to open-minded people. I realize, though, that now I'm talking about stuff that's "on the edge." First of all, I think this stuff is something that any honest teacher (if he or she is a sexual person at all) will admit happens. Hey, teachers get attracted to their students! If all this seems really offensive to you, it's probably because you're hearing it from a gay guy. I mean, come on. Shall we drop the hypocrisy here? This stuff goes on all the time! The big question, of course, is: should a teacher at a university level actually respond to the flirtations of the students? I mean, sure, there will be flirtations and attractions. But shouldn't they *not* respond? Doesn't it make the learning process better?

That's the whole point, here, and I don't take this issue lightly. I'm writing about teaching, not about sex.

Remember: you can't teach a person to be gay. By this I mean a child or a teenager is not an innocent slate upon which you write. You can't change them completely. I'm not saying that early (or adolescent) sexual experiences don't affect your sexual choices later. Apparently, the earlier these experiences happen the more effect they have. My first sexual experience was with my best boyfriend when I was seven. I remember we went to bed together one night. We were sleeping over as best buds.

Sex sure wasn't on my mind. I didn't know anything about sex then, I had no urges. But sure 'nuf, he woke up whatever I had. We frigged each other and looked at each other's dicks. It was so erotic. He was a lean, freckled boy, well-muscled, unlike me. But I guess he liked the chunky type. I remember the morning after, we were lying in bed together late. And we started frigging. And my dad poked his head in the bedroom door. I was so scared. I thought he was going to say, "You two faggots get out of bed!" But no, he didn't. He said—if you can believe it, and I'll never forget the words—"How are you doing, you two bathing beauties?" It was so neat. His remark seemed to tactfully encapsulate our nascent homosexual yearnings. Yes, we did feel like we were two "bathing beauties" and it was all young and silly and fun. I always loved my dad for saying that. And he seemed to be acknowledging the homosexuality that exists, to some degree, in all men.

Now I don't mean by this that all men are homosexuals. Even though the bigots sometimes think we mean that. That's where I think the bigots are really screwed up. They seem to think that fags want to take over the world and make everyone into a fag. How could they have so little faith in heterosexuality? Let me tell you, no matter how much proselytizing fags do, they could never switch over all the men in the world. Some men will always be straight, okay, so relax bigots, relax. (I thought it was really funny when I saw this show recently, on *60 Minutes*, all about Queer Studies courses at universities. It was one of those "investigative reports" that's supposed to weed out all the horrible corruption. Well, lo and behold, the corruption they found was that lots of universities have Queer Studies courses. And, as you might expect, these courses are taught by fags and dykes. The whole show was quite funny. They had these kids on and they picked the younger-looking ones for better effect. So they had this little, freckled, ponytailed, red-haired girl looking like a real Barbie-teen, and they're asking her, "Do you think it's important for you to learn about sadism and masochism?" And the girl goes, "Umm. I don't know." It was hilarious, the way they set up the teachers as being these proselytizing homosexuals and lesbians. All but tying up the students and whipping them with leather straps. Of course, St. Stephen's didn't have any Queer Studies courses. It being a very white little university with a religious name. It did have a Sexual Diversity course, but that was all bound up with feminism and female circumcision and didn't have much to do with sex. But I was there. Teaching *Theatre*. Let's face it, if you're trying to get rid of all the queer teachers, you're not going to do it just by getting rid of the Queer Studies courses. Sorry, Harry Reasoner. We're everywhere. And unfortunately, we can't make your kids queer anyway. We may wish we could, but, we can't!)

So, why can't you make someone gay? I think if you get someone really early (call it molestation or pederasty or whatever) you can influence them. For good or ill. I mean, it can turn them off or on being gay, one way or the other, depending on their very early experiences and inherited genetic inclinations. (It's all written up in this book *The Homosexual Matrix*, by this guy named Tripp, who used to work with Kinsey. Okay, he's a homosexual. But he's a very smart writer. Jeez.) The main thing to remember is that most doctors and psychologists say that by a very early age people's attractions have been decided. And though experience may add to this, there's nothing much that can be done about it.

You can't really molest a straight boy, in other words. He wouldn't let you. And if you tied him down and raped him, he would probably not choose to be a homosexual just because of it. It wouldn't be any fun. (But that's clearly not consensual, and that's not what we're talking about here.) What I'm trying to say is two things:

a) kids are sexual beings

b) by the time you get around to having sex with them—let's assume puberty—their sexual identity has already been created.

In fact, I think it's all the Victorian shit that makes the Alice-in-Wonderland-type kids into non-sexual beings. Victorianism sets them up as victims. If we refuse to acknowledge the sexuality of children and adolescents, then they become blank slates, ripe for molestation. But if we acknowledge that children are extremely sexual, they can no longer masquerade as innocents. And let's face it, half their appeal to the molester is suddenly gone. Hey, straight people, couldn't we finally break this Victorian pattern that sets up women and children as innocent? If you pretend women and children are innocent, that just makes them more eminently molestable. And they're not! Let me tell you a great way to make a molester impotent. *Desire* him. I'm not recommending this on an individual basis. I'm recommending this for us as a culture. If women and children are open about being predatory and desiring creatures, then the molesters in our culture have no more "innocents" to molest. I mean, look at what the press did to Monica Lewinsky during the whole Clinton fiasco. I just loved it the way they tried to make her look like this innocent little teenager that had been molested. Then you take one look at her and go: What teeth! What bazooms! What ambition!

I mean, I saw on *Hard Copy* that she had stalked one of her teachers at Lewis and Clark High School in Los Angeles. Give me a break. Monica Lewinsky was certainly old enough to know whether she wanted to give a blow job. And since President Clinton's dick was allegedly the same diameter as a quarter, it would have been a good size for her to start on. If she was interested in giving good blow jobs in the future.

I'm sorry to turn this into a lecture. But I'm sure a lot of you (if you're honest about it) probably felt like putting down this book when I started mentally raping my students. But my contention is that university students are not innocent—and that acknowledging fantasy is the first step to controlling it.

(Now, okay, *I* didn't ultimately control it. But that's actually because I changed my ideas about what education is. I don't think that real education can happen at a university any more. Also, I fell in love. But we haven't reached that part of the story yet.)

I didn't sleep with any of my students that summer, I just raped them in my mind and flirted with them. So leave me alone. All teachers do the same thing. In fact, your grocer probably does the same thing to you every day. And you ignore him and buy your oranges.

But that summer I figured that the only way I could control myself was to get a boyfriend. These kids were driving me crazy. So I had to find a boyfriend who was a student. But on the other hand, I still didn't think it was right for me to date one of my own pupils. I still had Matthew's edicts about denial echoing in my head. And the image of him at the window. Even though I didn't have any physical desire for Matthew anymore, I felt that I didn't want to disappoint him. And the fact that I never ever wanted to disappoint him may ultimately be what got me into trouble.

So I talked with my friend Lyle, who was, like, the only person who kept me alive in dull and dreary Stony Bay. All I can say is, something should be done about male tourists' legs in the summer. I mean, female tourists are just—well, they're not my cup of tea sexually. So they can dress as bag ladies for all I care. But, oh, those old pot-bellied guys in their plaid shorts on their way to the sailboat! The only way I would ever get that night-marish image out of my head was to have sex with a student. Even when I ran back to the city to forget, all I could think about was old guys and their boney knees. Which led to obsessive thinking about young guys and their furry thighs. And how I wasn't getting any of the real goodies. So I finally said, "Lyle,

I'm going crazy here!" I told him all about "The Three." He was very impressed. So I just asked him right out, "What would happen if I slept with one of my students?" He peered at me over his vodka and tonic. "I think you really should ask what would happen if you got caught!" "Yeah, okay, that then." "Well, Matthew has standards, it's a classy school, he wouldn't stand for it." "I might not get caught." "Yeah, but do you want to risk it?" "Lyle, I'm going crazy here." "I know, I know." And then an idea ocurred to me. "What if I slept with a student who wasn't one of my own?" This seemed to be a realistic compromise. "Oh, that's fine," said Lyle. "In fact, that's how a lot of professors deal with it. Just sleep with someone who is not now, nor ever will be, your student." "Would it be bad if they became my student?" "Well, it wouldn't be a good thing. But it's a lot better than sleeping with one of your own students." "Oh, okay." I could have kissed him. He made me feel a lot better.

The fact is, I felt that I was wasting the best part of myself that summer. All my life, I've slept with younger men, loved them, and taught them. And they've taught me things, too. So here I am, all of a sudden. I'm on this campus with all these beautiful young things. The type that could teach me a lot, and the type that I could learn a lot from. And I'm missing all that possible experience. Loving younger men is what I consider to be the best part of myself. The best of what I have to give. It is me. And simply because I'm a teacher, I'm going to waste the best I have to offer? I'm going to ignore all this positive energy?

And I know what you're thinking. You're thinking it's all about my dick. Well, yes. But it wasn't just that.

Okay?

My biggest relationship was with Steve. Steve is still alive somewhere. And Steve was my first boyfriend. And I was twenty-eight and he was seventeen. And even then I felt this man-boy thing. But he was the first man I ever had sex with, so it was a big production. I remember very much getting off with him on the first night. And I remember saying to him over and over again, "I don't know you. I don't know you." This was a big thing for me. As a teenager, I only had sex with women. Women who I knew very well and then supposedly fell in love with (except I didn't). And there I was, having much more passionate sex with someone I barely knew. (So my first gay experience was kind of an experience with a stranger. And yet, it was ecstatic. I think that had a future effect.) That was a big thing for me.

Steve, of course, had perfect thighs, with a round, hairy bum, which I used to lick and fuck. But that wasn't the whole story. Steve proved to be a very smart and witty young writer. And we started to write letters to each other every day. Even when we lived in the city together. We began to have a literary love affair. And Steve, of course, pretended he wasn't sure that he was in love with me (but I think he was). And in his spare time, he chased after big-butted Italians. (At the time he called them "Ginos.") And it would torture me. Because I couldn't imagine Steve ever having sex with anyone besides me. Because to me, he was my beautiful boy, forever, and he'd blessed me with his love. Then Steve went away to Europe and pretended to be a heroin addict. He was just playing, trying to scare me. (It's a "boy" thing.) I wrote him and told him that it was okay to commit suicide. (You should never contradict boys outright, even if they're acting really crazy.) We all commit suicide, I said. Every day, in fact. It all depends on how quickly you decide to kill yourself. The slow method is stuff like steak and cigarettes. The fast method is stuff like heroin and unsafe sex. I suggested he opt for the slow suicide that is the norm. I think he got my message. He stopped playing with heroin. (He sent me a sexy picture of himself holding up his arms. "See, no trackmarks, see?") And he sent me his jockstraps in the mail: I would smell them and wank off. And he sent me long stream-of-consciousness letters and we would discuss my obsessions in the letters. Pasolini, Frank O'Hara, and Lana Turner.

We loved each other to death. And we could spark each other, and miss each other passionately, and express that in our "letters" relationship. And he was everything to me. You see, just writing about him I start to get incoherent and smarmy, but it's all true. And then one day, Steve came back from Europe. We had written so many poems for each other that I thought he loved me for sure. But it was only a month after he came back when he broke up with me. I'll never forget it. We were sitting on a bench outside a hospital. And he just sat me down and told me, "Sorry, I can't sleep with you anymore." I died. I was inconsolable.

I went on a drunkslashstoned binge for months.

I discovered the baths.

I couldn't believe it. We were going to be forever, blah blah. Looking back on it now, it was all about what everyone expects from their first love. But at the time, I couldn't see it.

And what did I learn from Steve? I learned so many things I can't list them here. But the main thing I learned was that I was one hot guy. And I didn't learn that until ten years later. During all the time I was going out with Steve, I thought he was the beautiful young boy and I was the ugly older man. At least that's how I imagined it. But we took a little row of pictures of each other once at a train station in New York. And when I look at these pictures today, I think I look a lot cuter than him. In fact, I know I was cuter than him. Can you believe that? That's what obsessive love does to you—it makes you think you're not cute. And it's not true. I am cute (I have the photos to prove it.)

I don't know what Steve learned from me, but I know he's married to a blond boy now and they have a perfect love affair and he's still a writer and he writes stream-of-consciousness stuff like this sentence so I guess in fact he has learned something or at least I hope so.

And that's my little story about Steve. But I think you can see that these relationships are very special for me. And there's lots of back-and-forth learning besides the bumfucking and licking.

So am I to put all future "Steves" on the back-burner because I'm a teacher?

Because that's where I'd be most likely to meet him, of course. Some boy who wants to learn, or change, or act. I'd meet him at school.

I have a question. Would Steve have had the courage to become a writer if I hadn't fucked him up the bum (and also endlessly licked that gorgeous keester)?

I'll leave that seemingly preposterous question for now, but I'll come back to it later.

So, all this frustration built up. And two things happened at once that propelled me—yes—to have an affair with a student. Thank God, it wasn't one of my own.

The first was going out for drinks after one of the school events. I had a drink with this young, very attractive, straight, male teacher. I haven't mentioned him (Don) because I didn't know him very well. But he was very charming. He was a bit afraid of me, like all the other straight teachers there. But there we were in the university pub having a drink. And this straight (but handsome) forty-year-old teacher is chatting up one of his female students. And the student is like eighteen years old or something. And she's blonde and completely sexy. (Don't ask me how I know she was sexy. There are just certain cultural signals that mean sexy to straight men: blonde hair, big boobs that bounce, silly femininity, and a lack of clothing. You know—the clichés.) And she's chatting up this teacher and they're having a fine old time. And Don is talking to her about her belly button ring. Yes. I'm serious. The ring in her navel. She's going, "Do you like it?" and he's going, "Yes, it's very nice," and she's saying, "I think I should have gotten a smaller one," and handsome young Don goes, "That one's fine," and she goes, "Do you think so?" and he goes, "Well, you have a small belly button," and she goes, "You think I do?" and he goes, "Yes," and she goes, "Is that a bad thing?" And I just can't go on. You get the idea. Professor and student engaged in conversation. You get my drift? Now, for the two of them, this was a perfectly ordinary after-school conversation. And I'm thinking, why am I so guilty about having sex with a student? I mean, this guy is practically having sex with this girl's belly button. And you might say, "But he's not actually fucking her belly button," and I would say, "Who cares?" And I think that on some more profound level, this belly button chat may be education. And you can say, "Bullshit—what education?" And I can say, "For instance, this guy is respecting her, not molesting her, and she obviously idolizes him. And this guy is someone who teaches her (and is intelligent). And he's obviously attracted to her. But that's better than most dumb men who have probably just told her to shut up and suck it in the past." In other words, the combination of sexual attraction and the learning experience is actually important. It can be the most important part of learning.

And I thought, if this straight teacher can talk to a girl about the size of her belly button, I can have sex with a student. Especially if it's not my own student!

And the opportunity supplied itself in no time, in a surprising way. I was back at the Religious Studies library, because in my frustration I thought I'd look up St. Bernard (you know, the gay monk who presented himself to St. Stephen). I thought if I followed Matthew's lead and looked this stuff up, I might learn something that would help me with my dilemma. Well, I didn't even have time to wait for the old lady to get the books from the stacks, because who should appear? This guy who I fucked when he was fourteen!

I know that sounds shocking, but it's true. There I was, about to get this old book, when Montgomery sits down beside me. (I didn't know it was Montgomery at the time.) And he goes "Jack," and I go, "Yeah," and he goes, "Do you remember me?" and I go, "No." And I mean, why should I? What happened with him was so long ago. So Montgomery goes, in a whisper—remember we were surrounded by all the Divinity students—"Remember we had sex six years ago when I was fourteen?" And I said, "What, what are you talking about? I never had sex with anyone who was fourteen!" I was, admittedly, a little defensive, but wouldn't you be? I thought he was making it all up. Then I pondered the whole thing for a minute. And I remembered this Black kid. (Montgomery was Black.) You see, years ago when I came back from Amsterdam—I'm sure this happens to everyone—I was so high on Amsterdam sex and freedom that I decided to put this outrageous ad in the local gay newspaper. (That's really all those little fag newspapers are good for sometimes.) The ad said I was into all sorts of hot sex. I think I'd done a little fisting in Amsterdam, and I was feeling like a big top. (Those feelings come and go with me.) So anyway, Montgomery answered one of my ads. I remember when he came to my little apartment in the city. I was taken aback because he looked about twelve years old. Unfortunately, I still found him attractive. I asked him how old he was and he said, "Eighteen," and I figured I'd done my legal duty. So now it was time to do my sexual duty and fuck him. Which I'm pretty sure I did. I don't remember if any fisting went on. Looking at Montgomery in the Divinity library suddenly brought all these memories back to me. "Wait a minute. I remember a kid once. But the kid said he was eighteen." "That's what I told you then. But I lied," said Montgomery with a bit of a sweet smile. "So was it good?" I asked, always the provocateur. "Sure," he said, "it was fine." Fine is not my idea of sexual praise, but it was better than a kick in the head. So he goes, "We should get together sometime." "Sure," I said. "I'm a teacher here." This didn't seem to faze him at all. He gave me his number and we made plans to have lunch.

We decided to eat at this little coffee shop in town. Near one of the local touristy sailing shops. I remember I was so excited about having a date with a student. It felt right somehow, like something that I should be doing, like I wasn't wasting my time or myself on campus. It felt wonderful, actually. I thought, let someone see me. Lyle told me it was okay if this guy is not my student. He's not my student. Okay?

Montgomery told me he was a Divinity student, which I thought was great. He could help me research this St. Bernard stuff. Apparently, he had a goal: to be a gay priest. I talked to him about the fact that being an "out" gay priest was impossible. He had ideas about reforming the whole church, trying to stop the abuse from inside. It was really very admirable. We talked about sex and religion. I never really thought about sex and religion that much before. Montgomery said that when I talked about having sex with a student it sounded sort of like a religious quest.

This sort of piqued my interest, but I didn't think much about it at the time.

Montgomery and I didn't have sex right away. We'd go out in the city and cruise other people. Montgomery was very into threesomes and getting fucked by big guys. He had one big guy who was his favourite who he called "Mr. Much Man." The guy must have been three hundred pounds for sure. Montgomery was twenty and just basically horny all the time. That suited me fine. We fucked a couple of times. But I could tell he wanted threesomes. I'm not into that. My favourite thing about Montgomery was the way he would walk into bars when I was waiting for him. It was very pretty. Very moving. He walked into a gay bar with this embarassed little smile that said "Everyone is looking at me, and I know I'm going to have sex here tonight. Because, well, I'm hot!" It was really very sweet. I remember the days when I used to walk into bars feeling like that. You have to be pretty young (and pretty pretty) to walk into a gay bar like that everytime. Most of the time I walk into a bar thinking, "Oh my God, I've fucked everyone here. How boring." But sometimes there is still that sweet expectation, and I could see it in Montgomery.

Montgomery kept me happy for a while, and it really didn't feel like I was doing anything wrong. After all, he had been my lover way before St. Stephen's.

It was a crazy time for me. I was very happy. I got close to flirting openly with my students. I think the other teachers were still a bit suspicious of me. Because I wasn't fucking Matthew, I didn't have the "good education seal of approval" anymore. And I was really having a ball teaching. I loved telling the students all about my life (leaving out some X-rated stuff, of course). I remember one day that summer: it was during class and I was laughing, wearing shorts, and sipping on a root beer. The whole class had gone on a break. One of the older teachers leaned into the classroom for some reason. It was Hettie Prinsell. She didn't like me. And she saw me standing there alone, holding a bottle. "Where are your students?" she asked.

"Oh, they're on break," I said.

"I see," she said, stiffly. She pointed at my root beer bottle.

"Are you drinking?" she asked, archly, raising a brow.

"It's root beer," I said, waving the bottle in her gnarly, old face, feeling very gay, in every sense of the word. "See. Dad's." I thought the brand name was very appropriate, now that I was fucking one of the students at St. Stephen's. Hey, a Divinity student, too. She huffed away, pissed off that she wasn't able to catch me doing anything wrong. I think the whole of St.

Stephen's was hoping to catch me doing something wrong that summer, but it wasn't to be. The big shakeup wouldn't happen until the fall term, when I met Theodore.

But that's another, more secular story.

Part Two

L et me tell you about my favourite teachers. It seems to me they were my favourite teachers because they revealed something personal, something about their feelings, or their bodies, or both.

The first, the best teacher I remember, was Mr. Lavey. He taught me history from grade seven to nine. On some level, I was as in love with Mr. Lavey as I was with Miss O'Brian. I don't know if he knew it. He did encourage me to hang out with him, though.

In his history class, Mr. Lavey fostered controversy and argument—boy, did I like to argue. I was very opinionated about—well, I can't remember what. I think my views were pretty right-wing. I didn't get lefty until I became a homosexual and realized how oppressive life could be. But the point is, the whole class would just sit there like dumb thugs until I began to argue.

I really could stir things up. I think that's why Mr. Lavey liked me so much; it made his job easier. And I wrote these essays for him that were incredibly cheery and funny. They were supposed to be papers about the War of 1812 and stuff. But I'd give them great titles like "How to have a Stupid War and Alienate a Whole Bunch of People and Spend Lots of Money and Solve Nothing." And the essay would be organized like a conversation between two soldiers. And each of them would have empty pockets, say, complaining about how little money they had when the war was over and why. Looking back on it, these essays were incredibly creative. And Mr. Lavey loved them. And I would hang out with him after class and, well, I fell for him. He wasn't attractive in a traditional way. He was short and he looked something like a monkey with a pug nose. He had acne scars. But it didn't matter to me. And I'd tell Mr. Lavey that I was too unpopular and I wanted to quit being a brainer and try and get lower marks. We actually made that a project. For me to get lower marks. So he was sort of a friend, too, and psychotherapist. He came over to my house once. And he had dinner with my mom. I wanted like anything for them to get married. (My parents were divorced.) I mean, it made perfect sense to me! I thought of myself as Hayley Mills in *The Parent Trap*. I didn't realize that, of course, the only thing these two people had in common was that I loved them more than anything in the world.

Another great teacher I had was Mr. Manley. I had him in grade five. Mr. Manley was incredibly handsome and I had him for a whole year. It was hard for me to study because he was so cute and (even when I was ten) I was always imagining what he was like under his clothes. Well, I remember one day he said we were going to have a "special" class. He closed all the doors and windows and pulled the curtains and rolled up his sleeves. It was so exciting. He told us that this would be a very important day for all of us. I couldn't believe it. He said he was going to show us something very important. I was sure he was going to show us his dick. Absolutely convinced of it. I remember thinking at the time how educational that would be. He didn't, though. Instead, he took out a pack of cigarettes and smoked one. Right in front of us, in the classroom. He looked so sexy when he smoked. It was unbearable. Just like James Dean. And he was our teacher! And then he took a paper napkin and he breathed into the napkin after taking a smoke and showed us the mess of nicotine on the paper. And then he said, "This is what happens when you smoke. This is why you must never smoke." He was so serious. I almost came in my pants. And I remember thinking how privileged we were to see this side of Mr. Manley. The sincere, smoking side of him. It really was like seeing him naked. When it was over Mr. Manley opened the door again and rolled down his sleeves. I spent six years in elementary school. The only day I remember clearly in that whole time was when Mr. Manley rolled up his sleeves and smoked. He showed me something of himself. I wish he showed me more. (By the way, I didn't start smoking until I was almost thirty years old. Which means my skin is very clear and unwrinkled for an older guy. Was this due to Mr. Manley? You be the judge.)

And then there was Mr. Quelch. He's still alive. That's what I have to say about Mr. Quelch. He's still alive and I still see him now and then in the gay ghetto.

Mr. Quelch was my music teacher. When I was about seventeen years old I used to play in a quartet at music school. (It's where I met Marco, the handsome and romantic trumpet player.) I pursued music quite seriously for a while before I started acting. I played the cello. And Mr. Quelch used to teach us how to play the Schubert "Trout" quintet every Saturday morning. I remember it was a bright, sunny room with windows all around, and empty music stands. Charming orchestral paraphernalia was everywhere. I loved getting up early and dragging my cello to practice. I don't know why, considering Mr. Quelch was such a horrible man, a sadist. He was about sixty years old at the time. This was thirty years ago. And he's still alive! But even at that time he was all bent over and bald. He was your nightmare music teacher. You'd play, like, one note and he'd go, "No, no no!" And he'd make you do it again. And again, and again and again. Until you never wanted to hear that note again. He made me hate the "Trout" quintet. (Even today, I can't listen to it without getting tense. And I'm a Schubert freak.) He treated you like you were totally stupid. He was very easily exasperated. I hated him. But I also felt sorry for him because he just seemed so terribly unhappy. You couldn't make old Quelch smile, ever. And his whole life was music. Everything. And it seemed like he was tuned into another world, a world that was somewhere in his brain, where every note was played perfectly, by someone, but not you. Because every note had to be *right*.

So that would have been the whole story, but I inadvertently and advertently learned other stuff about Quelch. First, I asked some people at the music school about him. And they said that Quelch had been a child prodigy. And that something had happened (an unexplained tragedy) that caused him to never fully realize his potential. I always wondered what happened. But it expained his bitterness.

And later, as an adult, when I became a total faggot, I was lying in a room in the most depraved bathhouse in the city. And who should come cruising by my room but a very, very old Mr. Quelch. You have to realize that this bathhouse was where people would pee on people, and tie each other up, and do various other indignities. And there was old Quelch, who must have been eighty-five, hobbling around, all bent over. It all made sense then. He was a sadist, in art and in life. I'm sure he tied people up and made them beg for things. And when they begged wrong he'd make them do it again and again until they got it right.

Those are the three teachers, that is, *real* teachers who showed me part of their life and helped me to learn.

There were two other people in my life I want to tell you about who also taught me stuff. But they weren't hired to teach me. They just did. Kate and Michael.

Kate was this S/M dyke that I met because I moved into this group house once. She lived there part-time. I remember being afraid of her. The guys in the house said, "Oh, a dyke lives here part of the time and her name is Kate. And you'll really like her, she makes porn movies." At the time, I didn't know any dykes and I was basically scared of them. Kate changed all that. She was probably the funniest person I ever met. She was a professor of political philosophy and she made porn movies for fun. When I first met her, she asked me if I was a "top" or a "bottom." I said I didn't know. She said, "When you have sex, do you like to do all the work, or do you like to have someone do all the work?" I said, "They can do all the work, that's fine with me." Then she said, "Do you like to come up with the fantasies and the ideas for great sex, or do you want your partner to do that?" And I said, "Someone else can do that, thank you." Then she said, "Well, you're a bottom then." It was very interesting to find that out. Then she gave me some advice. She said, "Since you're a masochist, just don't tell a lot of people, except the ones you want to fuck. First of all, there are too many masochists in the world anyway. Secondly, you'll get treated badly when you wait in line. (She meant any old line, like at the grocery store.) People find out you're a bottom and they'll make you go to the end of the line." It was good advice. (Nowadays I don't know what I am. I think maybe I'm an active bottom or a submissive top.) She also told me I was a "pervert." "What's that?" I asked. She said it just meant that I was a sexual person. And that sex was of prime importance to me. She said she was a pervert, too. She used to hang out with female street hookers who were usually quite beautiful and sometimes a little tragic and dangerous. She taught me a lot. Then, years later, I was over at her house and we were having a party and she was trying to get me to fuck her friend (male, very cute). And we were staggering around and all stoned. And this guy and I peed together. She watched, and the next morning she told me that my dick was really great.

I don't know why, but it seemed like a special kind of bond to have with a lesbian. And it made me feel really good about myself that she liked my dick.

Then there's Michael. Can't talk about him really. Except he makes me think of Theodore (in a way). I think maybe Theodore was the incarnation of Michael for me. Enough to say Michael was a boy I loved. He was a crazy, punk, ex-hooker brat. He did too many drugs and got AIDS. And we used to fuck occasionally, in strange places (toilets in restaurants, for instance). One day, we were looking for pot desperately, and we couldn't find any. So we just used some tea from the cupboard and smoked it. And suddenly everything got so slow. Very slow. I remember crossing a very small field and just never getting to the other side. Afterwards, when Michael was gone (he eventually died), I tried to figure out what fucking tea that was. A tea that you can find in any cupboard that makes you completely stoned out of your mind. Of course, I couldn't find the damn tea. Maybe it didn't exist. What did we get high on? Only Michael knows, and he's not around.

When he was dying in San Francisco he phoned me and I didn't know what to say. Literally. I could hear he was all drugged up. Michael was always completely stoned and wounded, and I always wanted to help him. But there isn't much you can do sometimes. Michael completely accepted me. We loved each other in a totally relaxed way, whenever we felt like it, sometimes sexual, sometimes non-sexual. I remember Michael once wanted to fuck me without a condom. He just wanted to shove his big hard dick up my ass so badly. He was going to use spit. "Spit and push," he said. "Remember the old spit and push? I like the old spit and push..." I didn't let him. And so I didn't get AIDS then, at least. (I never get tested so I don't know whether I have it now.)

At the beginning of the fall term at St. Stephen's, they gave me stupid Beginners Acting and Advanced Acting to teach again. I thought it was some sort of conspiracy—I thought they were trying to get me to teach nothing but very attractive students. I know this is paranoid, but I figured it was a test. A test directly from Matthew. And the first day of classes, I remember thinking that one of the students— he wore a baseball cap—was particularly slender and lovely. But it was hard to see him because of his cap. When I went through roll call he raised his hand. When I read out "Theodore Strong" he said, "Call me Todd." "Okay," I said. It was no big deal. I noticed that his voice was very deep and kind of sexy. That's all I noticed.

The next day of class, Todd was wearing his cap but it was turned around, and I could see his face. He was very "boy" handsome and terribly thin. He never ever looked healthy. And he had those little lines around his mouth that some boys and some men have that accent the lips.

His lips deserve a paragraph to themselves. They were full and pouty, the lips of a girl. They made him look girlish. But there they were, on a boy's face, next to the stubble of his boy cheek. You just wanted to kiss them.

His eyes were blue and he had long lashes, of course. His hair was thin: that's why he wore a cap—he had hair that was too old for his face. With the cap, he looked about fourteen years old. Without the cap, his head and face were unplaceable in years. Ageless. He was either a wizened boy or a very, very young old man.

I haven't done him justice. His body (which I wouldn't see until later) was, of course, very thin. A boy's body, with just that perfect hair distribution. And he had this way of walking that was very aristocratic. His long arms and fingers swayed slightly when he walked, but his spine and head were very erect. He walked with a strange and subtle dignity.

I began to realize that Todd was very different, not like other students. In fact, it was hard to believe he was a student at all. (Part of me will never really believe he was a student. Instead, it seems that he was dropped into my class by some sort of happy accident, or by fate, or by a trick of Matthew's.) First of all, he didn't seem to be an upper-class kid. Sure, he walked like an aristocrat, but he usually wore overalls and a cap. (Overalls must be the sexiest clothes ever invented. But we won't go into that now.) I found out later he actually was from an upper-class background—or claimed to be. You never knew with him. But he just seemed kind of wacky. He didn't have any of the reserve of the upper-class wasp kids. He answered questions with off-the-cuff, honest answers. Very real. He didn't seem to be very educated. He said that William Inge's *Bus Stop* was "sort of corny." He said that Eugene O'Neill "talked too much." Now these were certainly what old Lisa Lamprey-Pistoli would have called "undergraduate" responses. But he *was* an undergraduate. And they made sense, really.

I also noticed that he didn't seem to have any friends in the class. This was the other odd thing. Most students bond with each other long before they bond with a teacher. For some reason, Todd seemed to harbour no hope of ever bonding with the other students. It was as if the other students weren't there, so he immediately bonded with me.

It happened pretty quickly.

There was another thing about him. He was very much the "boy." Let me say this about straight boys, and even some gay ones: by the time they get to the age of my students (let's say over eighteen), they start to want to act like men. (In most cases, they started acting like men way before age eighteen.) They start to hang around in that butch-daddy way. They don't want to show weakness. They don't want to be cute. Occasionally, they act cute when cute girls are around. But basically they're really concerned with being men.

Now, it's not that Todd was effeminate. It wasn't that. (I wouldn't have minded if he was. In fact, he made a lousy drag queen.) It's just that when his eyes searched me out in class, they looked at me the way a little boy looks at a man. Like a puppy.

I don't think the other kids liked him. They seemed to sense that he was different somehow. These kids who went to St. Stephen's, well…the girls were either going to get married, or they were going to go on to professional careers, or to teaching. The boys were all going to be professionals. Todd was definitely *not* going to be a professional. (He already was a professional, in a way.) But for these upper-class kids to hang out with him? No, I couldn't see it happening. He was very lonely. So was I. So it was inevitable that I would get to know him better. And I did.

One day, he wanted to talk to me during my office hours. I had office hours once a week and usually I just sat there, twiddling my thumbs. During this time, students are supposed to come and talk to their professors. Students never came to talk to me. But I put that down to my good teaching. I figured I was so approachable in class that they didn't need a special time. Occasionally, some whiney girl or boy would come and try to con me into giving them extra time to finish things. Pat told me not to let them con me, and I didn't. Probably the students realized I was pretty unmanipulatable. So, they never took advantage of my office hours.

The office was small and wood-panelled, with huge windows, like in the mansion where Matthew—well, you remember. I always left the door open when I had office hours. I figured that way I couldn't get into any trouble.

Todd came to talk to me about a scene from *Tea and Sympathy*. That's the famous (not very good) play by Robert Anderson. I say it's not very good because it doesn't have much to say. It does bring traditional gender roles into question, but in a half-hearted way. (Actually, I don't know why I put scenes from the play on the course. Maybe it's because it had a great effect on me when I was a kid. And I thought it would be good to have the young actors try their hand at a scene from a historic gay play.) I don't know if you know it. Deborah Kerr played the lead in the movie. She plays the wife of a teacher at a boys' university. She is very sweet and nice and she gives the boys tea and sympathy in the afternoons (she has little chats with them). Well, this one boy is always being kidded because people say that he's a homosexual. He's very effeminate and plays the guitar (apparently a sure sign of homosexuality in the fifties). Anyway, she has one of her little "tea and sympathy" talks with the boy and ends up fucking him and reassuring him of his heterosexuality. In a way, it's a pretty horrible message. So the play makes an interesting discussion point for class.

I remember finding it kind of ironic that this boy that I was so attracted to would bring this play to me to discuss. Never mind the fact that it was such a simple play to understand. It wasn't *Mourning Becomes Electra* or something.

I was sitting behind the desk reading Northrop Frye. Actually, I thought reading Northrop Frye would make me look intimidating. Also, Frye always made me feel old and boring. For some weird reason I thought it was important to be as boring as possible that afternoon. You see, I had a feeling something crazy might happen. And I was right. It did.

Well, Todd bounces into the room and sits down. It's fall,

so he's wearing a pair of long, crazy cut-off shorts that make him look adorable because they're too big for him. He's wearing his cap turned around and he looks about twelve. He takes the book out of his knapsack and slams it down on the desk. "I don't get it, Sir," he says. I quell my immediate impulse to ask him not to call me Sir. For some reason, I have a feeling that with Todd, if he addresses me as "Sir," it might get complicated. I just launch in. "What don't you get, Theodore?" I used his real name for some reason, I don't know why. He looked so vulnerable and cute. He didn't look like a "Todd." "I told you to call me Todd," he said, with an appealing frown. "But your name is Theodore." "Everybody calls me Todd." I didn't know what he was talking about. I'd never heard anyone in class call him anything. "Okay, Todd, what don't you get?" (From this point on, I'll call him Theodore. It's very complicated. You see, Todd was Theodore's professional name. I didn't know that at the time. But I thought, I'll call him Theodore because Todd Strong sounds like a porn-star name. It was much harder to think of him as being like any other student with his porn-star name.) Theodore. Theodore.

"I don't get it," said Theodore.

"You'll have to be more specific."

"I mean this play seems to be about something, but the writer doesn't seem to want to talk about it."

"What does it seem to be about?"

"Well, the guy's a fag, right?"

Usually the students don't use the word fag. When Theodore uses it, he uses it the way other gay men use it. Fag is a word that only fags are allowed to use with each other. Otherwise, it is a form of abuse. The way Theodore used it, it was as if we were both a part of the club.

"I think he's a boy with gay feelings" I said.

"You think what?" said Theodore. He stood around. He

sort of bounced around in his sneakers, unable to keep still.

"I said, I think he's a boy with gay feelings."

"Oh, I get it," he said. "A boy. With gay feelings."

"Yes."

"Are you a boy with gay feelings?"

"What?" I said. He had completely caught me off guard. I didn't know what to say.

"I asked you, are you a boy with gay feelings?"

I immediately stood up and shut the door. Looking back on things, it was a very stupid thing to do. But it was an impulsive move.

As soon as I locked the door, Theodore ran to the highest point in the room. It was very strange. There was an old cart that used to have a television on it, parked in the corner. He ran over to another desk, climbed on top of it, then climbed up to the top of the cart and stood there, shivering as if it was cold. His shoes were at my chest height. He was on the other side of the room.

"Oh, why are you closing the door? Why are you closing it? Are you going to molest me? Oh, please sir, please don't molest me. If you molest me, I'll call the dean, I promise I'll call the dean. Don't molest me."

I stared at him from my seated position. I could not believe my eyes or ears.

"Sit down, please."

"I will not sit down. I won't sit down, you can't make me; are you going to make me?"

"I'm asking you to sit down."

"No, I'm scared."

He made little shivering sounds and noises. He was performing for me. It was very funny. I was a teacher. I wasn't supposed to react. And I suppose if I hadn't at that moment responded to Theodore's infectious fun, then things would have been very different. The thing to do would have been to leave the room. To open the door and walk out and never find myself alone with Theodore again. I did not do that, however. I sat at my desk, feeling very trapped in my role as "teacher."

"I'm asking you politely, one final time. Sit down."

"I won't sit down, I won't, I won't, I won't, I won't, I won't!" He stamped his feet in the corner. He was standing near the ceiling. The image was so incredibly ridiculous that I started to laugh. It was a kind of hysterical laughter, hard to describe now. I guess I was letting out months and months of frustration, sexual and general. Looking back, it makes me think of Matthew's drunken laughter that night in the mansion. Sort of helpless, coming from a very deep and vulnerable place. After all my agonies over my feelings of lust for students, how incredibly odd to have a student standing on the top of a video cart shouting, "No, no, no," resisting my imagined advances. It was a sort of surrealistic image. I laughed good and long, and I think it was an incredible release.

Theodore was immediately pleased and started to perform more enthusiastically.

"What, did I do something funny? Did I amuse you? Am I being funny? A funny guy? Tell me, I'm trying to be serious; you have to tell me tell me now. Why are you laughing?" He started to mock cry. "Why are you laughing? Please, I beg you! Tell me. Why are you laughing?" He jumped down on to the floor and lay on the floor, banging on my desk like a supplicant. "Why are you laughing at me? Tell me, why are you laughing?" He burst into mock tears and banged my desk as I continued laughing hysterically.

Well. Where to go from here? I didn't think about it. I was relieved to be laughing at last. Theodore continued his little performance and my laughter gradually wound down. When it was over, he was sitting in the chair opposite me again.

I thought maybe we could start over. There was a pause, and I thought: we can turn back now. Theodore never said the word "fag." He never climbed up to the ceiling. He never made me laugh so helplessly. He'll ask me intelligent questions about *Tea and Sympathy*. But what intelligent question was there to ask? Hadn't I assigned the scene in hopes that a student like Theodore might ask me a flirtatious question? Could I ever turn back now?

Theodore looked at me and I looked at him, and I knew some boundary had been crossed. We sat there for a moment, just looking at each other. It seemed that the whole of St. Stephen's was quiet, too, just waiting for us.

Then Theodore made a funny face. "I think you're hot," he said, just like that. "I think you're hot."

I was, again, totally unprepared. How does one react to this with dignity? As a teacher? I'm sure other teachers who have been in this situation have calculated a "bon riposte" that would change the subject completely. For instance, maybe I should have said, "No, I'm not." Except that I knew I was, and oh, how I wanted to hear it from a pretty boy like Theodore. Also to say, "No, I'm not," would obviously be accepting the subject of my attractiveness as a proper subject for discussion. That would not do. Again, what was the proper decorum for a professor in this situation? I decided I should open the door and ask him to leave. I did not. He said it again.

"I think you're hot."

It's hard to describe how he said it. In sort of a cloying fashion, mocking what he was saying. Very camp. Acting a bit like a little boy and a movie star. It was absolutely my sense of humour. I was completely captivated.

"You shouldn't be talking like that. I'm your teacher."

I stood up. He stood up. I was going for the door, really, I was.

"I think you should leave."

"Okay." He walked ahead of me towards the door. When he got to the door he turned his back to it and looked at me. Then he scrunched his face up, very unattractively, and sort of played with his shirt. "I think you're hot," he said again. Then he looked at me like a puppy. "Sorry, I do."

I should have opened the door. I know I should have opened it. Instead, I kissed him.

It was a fabulous kiss. With all that Theodore and I ever did, kissing was the best. He was a little boy kissing a man. It was very romantic. He gave himself up, sort of whimpered and acquiesced. He was submissive. And he wanted my large body, my arms, to envelop him. And all the while, there was the incredible feeling of my lips on his. At last, to caress that pout, that little-boy rose.

The kiss lasted a long time. And there was some writhing, with me sort of pinning him to the door. Later, I imagined Hettie Prinsell (the professor who hated me), creeping by, ready to report my indiscretion.

When it was over, we just sort of looked at each other. We were each a bit astonished, I think, by the intensity of the kiss. It's always amazing when two people seem to fit together like that, so effortlessly. Most surprisingly when they are, yes, basically strangers.

He gave me a little-boy look and then slipped out from between my arms and opened the door.

"Excuse me," he said. And then he slipped out. I watched him walk down the hall. He was doing this mock sneaky thing, walking carefully down the hall. He turned and looked at me before he turned the corner and mimed "Shhhhh!" Then he was gone.

L et me pause for a minute here. Everybody take a breath. There. So.

I guess the thing is: I had kissed a student. Passionately.

Tongues, the whole thing. We had really kissed. But all was not lost. Not yet.

I mean, I could turn back. No one had to know. And more than that. It wasn't so awful what I had done. No elderly, lecherous pedant here. I had been attacked. Essentially. By someone who was at least as sexually knowledgeable as myself. That's for sure.

It seemed to me that it was my choice now.

A part of me wanted very badly to talk all this out with Matthew. Which is strange, because I knew exactly what he would say. But then again, it was not strange at all; I imagined he could save me.

What was in my mind was a talk Matthew and I had about a sacred trust.

And it seemed to me, of course, that Theodore was perhaps (beneath all his bravado) much more innocent than he seemed at first kiss.

The sacred trust is that all students are innocent. All students are precious. All students deserve the same respect: that we will not become involved with them in a physical way.

I thought of all the girl students (girls brought out this feeling in me mostly) who looked so vulnerable and innocent. I thought of fathers that probably yelled at them and called them stupid. It seemed to me that for some kids, being at university was their first chance to escape the stifling world of their parents. It may be their first time to be treated with respect. Wasn't it our duty as teachers not to complicate our relationship with them, at the very least?

Teenagers act older than they are. They assume a maturity in spite of, or because of, their sexual experience that we might mistake for self-respect. In fact, Theodore, for example, could have been an abused boy who desperately needed to meet a gay man who would not respond to his advances. A man who he could be friends with. A mentor.

My second meeting with Theodore confirmed all this, yet challenged it. The meeting was, of course, at his insistence. He wanted to talk about a scene from Edward Albee's *Who's Afraid of Virginia Woolf?* Well, that's a good thing, I thought. His taste in closeted American playwrights is getting better. (I know Albee came out of the closet later in life, but it was only after he got caught having sex in a park.) I decided that we would meet in a college café called The Aardvark. It was a cool and funky place with contemporary music. And it was run as a student co-operative business. The service was terrible, but the food was good. And I thought, at least Theodore won't jump over the table and attack me! And I was right, he didn't.

Theodore was late. I was already eating my omelette when made a little gesture to me as he hurried in. It was a very gay gesture. This was disconcerting to me.

He sat down, juggling a very large and eclectic meal on his tray. There certainly was something from every food group.

The talk about Albee quickly became a little "one man show" from Theodore. I asked him to tell me a little about himself, and I quickly learned that his cheerful, mocking exterior was a mask that hid a very troubled young life. (I know I sound like a social worker here. Well, I was trying to be one. I was trying to look at Theodore objectively and not obsess about his beauty and body hair.) Theodore was very glib about his life and he seemed proud of his troubles. This could all have been (probably was) a show.

Then, of course, comes the question. How much of what he told me was true?

In my view, it doesn't really matter. At the time, I thought: if there's a pathology here, it could be the pathology of abuse. Or maybe Theodore just has a very vivid imagination. Or to put it less charitably, maybe he's a liar perched precariously on the verge of schizoid fantasy. Either way, Theodore is fucked.

So here goes.

The first thing Theodore told me was that he was missing part of his nose. This was certainly an interesting anatomical fact. He asked me if I wanted to see it. I told him I did not. Apparently, it was something called the "septum." I wasn't sure of its use, but Theodore seemed fine without it. (Was a "septum" like an "appendix"?) The missing septum was due to coke abuse. And I don't mean the soft drink. But Theodore didn't do coke anymore. Or so he said.

Theodore told me that his parents were rich and that his mother was a photographer, and that he was living with them in Bunionville (yes, that's really the name), a very small town that was exactly halfway between Stony Bay and the city. He came from a big family with six brothers and sisters. He cheerily talked about his years of coke abuse, and how he almost died. And then he talked cheerily about his parole officer. (I'd never known anybody with a parole officer before—this was certainly educational for me!) He talked about his abusive ex-boyfriend, named Big Bob, who was a producer for a local radio station in the city. Bob had started him on coke. He talked about the fact that he had been a stripper in a gay bar in the city. He talked about his dad, who was gay, too. His dad's name was Butch.

Butch.

Butch didn't live with Theodore's mother anymore. He designed windows in a big department store. And Theodore and his Dad went to gay bars together. He talked about how there were sometimes some problems with Butch, who "got mad." He didn't elaborate on it at the time.

Apparently, Theodore had an agreement with his mother. The agreement was that if he agreed to go to school and finish his degree in Fine Arts, she would try and help him get a job in television. Theodore had worked at Big Bob's radio station before they broke up. So possibly Theodore could continue on with a career in broadcasting if he could get his degree.

The choice for Theodore was clear. Either he could stay in school, stay off the coke, and have a career in the media. Or he could go back to stripping, Big Bob, and the coke.

And lose his nose altogether, apparently.

So that was Theodore's story.

I was slightly aghast, but I tried to make it look like my omelette was too spicy. All during my eating, Theodore kept commenting on the way I ate.

"I love the way you eat. I could just sit all day and watch you eat."

"I'm a pig," I said, aware of my bad eating habits.

"No, you eat like you like it, it's great. I love a guy who really enjoys his food. You have to let me make you dinner sometime."

"I don't know if that would be appropriate."

"I really like watching you eat."

He did, actually, study me when I ate.

And that was my first lunch with Theodore.

As we were about to leave, we were putting our trays away and Theodore said, "Hey, can I come and visit you at your place in the city?"

"How do you know I live there?"

"I just know."

"No."

"Why not?"

"I'm a teacher and you're a student."

"Okay, then what if I quit school? Could I come and see you then?"

"Theodore, don't quit school."

"Well, if that's the only way you'll let me come to your apartment then I might just have to."

"Please don't quit school, it would make me very unhappy if you quit school."

"You don't like me very much, do you?"

"I didn't say that."

"Then why can't I come to your apartment?"

"Let's talk about this another time."

"Can we have lunch tomorrow?"

"What about the day after that?"

"Okay."

I had put him off for one more day.

It really did seem that I had enough information to make a reasoned, informed decision. A first reading of Theodore and his history seemed to make it very clear that he was a victim of abuse. And the abuse all seemed related to older men. First, there was a dad called "Butch." Now, I hate extrapolating a whole bunch of stuff just from somebody's name, but, *really*. How could any responsible sort of human being be called "Butch"? And then there's what Theodore said about him: "He's a nice guy. He gets mad sometimes. But he's a nice guy." This seemed to me to be a cover-up. And I couldn't help thinking that if his dad was gay, then he might have molested him. I know that sounds totally homophobic. But his name was "Butch." How could you treat anyone as a dad with a name like that?

Then there was Big Bob. If there's anything in the world I detest, it's an older fag who uses drugs to seduce a younger one. And it's all over the gay map. Look at Theodore. Missing part of his nose. All because some old faggot couldn't keep his boy interested without shoving coke up his nose while he's fucking him. Well, I didn't need coke. I could keep Theodore interested. I knew I could.

But there we go.

It's obvious that Theodore woke up the dad in me, the caregiver. The big question was this: what would be the best way to help him? Because I realized that I should try and answer that question without my dick getting in the way.

And I certainly wasn't going to let his threat to leave school affect me. Except that it did. A part of me just wanted to follow this line of thought: Jack, listen. He said he'd leave school if you didn't sleep with him. So you'd better sleep with him. But then I thought, maybe I'd better say, "No, I won't sleep with you," and see if he does actually leave school. I bet he's just testing me. I bet he won't leave.

But that didn't address the bigger picture. I should do whatever is best for Theodore, not what's best for me. Would it be better for Theodore to have a sexual relationship with me or not?

And then, of course—to really mix things up—there was the clear, unquestioned, visceral knowledge that I was in love with Theodore.

I had only known him for a month. And for two weeks of that month, I had been his teacher. Lately, I had gotten to know him a little better. But I knew him well enough to be certain that he was absolutely alive, entertaining, dangerous, smart, sexy, and perfectly poised—on the edge of something. On the edge of growing up, it seemed.

What to do with Theodore?

I probably did the wrong thing. I decided to turn to the Bible.

It wasn't a strange decision, really, if you think about it.

First of all, Matthew had started me in that direction, what with telling me about St. Stephen and St. Bernard. And I was still friends with Montgomery. With the advent of Theodore, it had become more of a friendship with Montgomery. So he loaned me his special Divinity student library card.

First I decided to try the Internet. I found a Catholic Web site and I e-mailed them a question about St. Bernard. The woman at the Catholic Web site was very cheerful (Ginnie!) and she told me that they had lots of information about St. Bernard in a library somewhere in Texas. She ended her e-mail with a perky "God bless you!"

Ginnie kinda scared me. I decided to try the old lady at the Religious Studies library at St. Stephen's first.

I looked up St. Bernard in Butler's *Lives of the Saints* and it contained some interesting passages. It mentioned his sermons on the Song of Songs. It also mentioned his later life: "...and it was at this period that he first met St. Malachy of Armagh; the ensuing friendship between the two lasted until Malachy's death in Bernard's arms nine years later," and he was called, "Doctor Mellifluus, the Honey-sweet Doctor."

Doctor Mellifluus. I liked that. If I was ever a doctor, that's what I would want to be called.

This wasn't enough. I was spending hours and hours in the library because I thought it would save me. I didn't know why.

And then the answer came.

I got the *Catholic Encyclopedia* and looked up saints. I was hoping to find something about St. Bernard and St. Malachy. Their relationship certainly sounded interesting. Well, the encyclopedia didn't even list Malachy as a saint. I guess he wasn't important enough. I mean, St. Bernard has his own day and everything. But it was something later on, something in the definition of the "Requirements of Sainthood" that caught my attention. It said that the main paths to sainthood were sacrifice and miracles and something else. (I can't remember what, but I do remember that at this point I was getting so excited I actually had to put down my pen and paper.) It also said there was one more path to sainthood. It was "love." They talked about the many kinds of "love." And then they talked about "human love." (I figured it was the closest those Catholics could get to talking about sex in their encyclopedia.) And sure enough, there were apparently only two religious figures in the whole history of world religion who ever reached sainthood through exploring "human love." One of them was some Arab guy and the other one was—you guessed it—St. Bernard.

He was beginning to remind me of the dog, the old faithful one that turns up when you need him.

It was time to try and find these sermons on the Song of Songs. Thank God I had Montgomery's "extra privileged" card, because it took the old lady about half an hour just to find them.

She was really nice about it, though.

What she brought me was four separate volumes of sermons on the Song of Songs. I began to devour them.

It said, in the introduction: "To appreciate the meaning of all this, as well as to grasp the profound meaning of the Song it is *better to love than to study*. As Bernard says: Holy love is the only subject treated in this Song. We must remember that love reveals itself, *not by words or phrases, but by action and experience*. It is Love which speaks here, and if anyone wished to understand it, *let him first love*. Otherwise it would be folly to read this song of love, *because it is absolutely impossible for a cold heart to grasp the meaning of language so inflamed*."

There was no doubt about it. This "Doctor Mellifluus" was talking about one thing only. The same thing my old fart of a teacher at university taught me. That you can't just learn from books. You have to go from books to life, and then back to books again.

I read on.

Let me tell you something about this St. Bernard guy. He was a real, true artist. These rants are supposed to be sermons, but hey, they're a lot more than that. I mean, if you compare him to Roland Barthes, they are on the same track. I don't know if you've ever read Roland Barthes's fabulous novel in the form of an essay, *A Lover's Discourse*. It's great. It's all about the words of love and what they do to us and how they affect us. But if you read between the lines, it's a story about Barthes and a boy. At least to me it is. Likewise, these "sermons" by St. Bernard were a lot more than just sermons. These weren't the

old sit-down-while-I-tell-you-a-parable-about-St.-Joseph-of-
Pultz-that-will-be-an-allegory-for-your-own-life variety of sermons. Oh no. These were detailed analyses of text. Almost
postmodern, these sermons take the Song of Songs word for
word. They try and analyze these words for their meaning. Now,
of course, they look at it all in a Christian context. And yet,
read it and you think, hey, this Christian named St. Bernard
definitely knew how to fuck. And it's all so gay!

There's this one chapter called "The Kiss." It's all about the
kiss that God gives to you—the kiss of faith or wisdom or
religion or whatever. And old St. Bernard, he insists that this
kiss is a real kiss, not a metaphor. You can tell he really doesn't
want you to think it's a metaphor. And he always wants to be
really sure that kiss is man to man. Listen:

"I must ask you to try to give your whole attention here. The
mouth that kisses signifies the Word who assumes human nature, the one mediator between God and mankind, himself a
man, Christ Jesus. It is for this reason that none of the saints
dared say; 'let him kiss me with his mouth,' but rather 'with the
kiss of his mouth.'"

But old St. Bernard isn't afraid to say:

"A fertile kiss therefore, a marvel of stupendous self-abase-
ment that is not a mere pressing of mouth upon mouth; it is
the uniting of God with man. Because in him were hidden 'all
the jewels of wisdom and knowledge.' I do not rise up, I am
not awakened, I am not shaken out of the dust, nor do I breathe
in hope, if the Prophet himself does not come down and kiss
me with the kiss of his mouth. Let him establish a covenant
with me, an everlasting covenant with me by the kiss of his
mouth... If he will not revoke his given word, let him empty
himself, let him humble himself, let him bend to me and kiss
me with the kiss of his mouth."

Let him bend to me and kiss me with the kiss of his mouth.

Pretty sensual stuff, eh? I'd like to just say that I rest my case here. Okay. I am aware that there are lots of little reference numbers in the text all around this passage. And I'm also aware that they probably lead to footnotes to assure you that old St. Bernard was not having an attack of homosexualitis. I'm sure the footnotes remind us that he was just being poetical or something. But I don't buy that. There are so many gay images in this text. And St. Bernard is so intent on making you realize that this kiss is not just the word of God, but that it actually entails kissing Jesus. A guy. One guy to another guy. Because the disciples were all guys, right? At the very least, St. Bernard is using sexual imagery—the way the Song of Songs did—to shock us into recognizing how beautiful, sensual, and important and immediate the kiss of God is.

Well, I have to admit I sort of thought when I kissed Theodore it was the kiss of God.

And that was where I got into real trouble.

I mean, why should it be the kiss of God, why should it? And who's God, him or me?

Well, why shouldn't it be the kiss of God? You know, old St. Bernard believed he was a saint because God kissed him. But we all know, from reading this passage, that the kiss of God is actually the kiss of Christ—a man. And Malachy died in Bernard's arms.

And there was one more thing about Theodore, one more thing I forgot to tell you.

Besides missing a septum, he had one more thing wrong with him. He had a weird spot on the left-hand side of the same nose. And I asked him about it. And he said, "Oh, it's this lesion. I hope it goes away."

That's the word he used—lesion.

Later on, the whole possibility of Theodore's having a disease, or specifically, *the* disease, came up. He had other symptoms, too, lumps and things.

But at the very least, Theodore was sick with something. He was sick with his coke addiction. Or his lack of self-esteem. Or the cliché gay sickness—AIDS. He was sick. He needed my help. Just like Malachy needed the help of St. Bernard.

That's what made me think that our kiss was something special and mystical. After all, how did St. Bernard know that he had gotten the kiss of God? He just said so. Well, I could just say that Theodore was my Malachy and our kiss was the kiss of God, too. Because it just seemed that way to me. With every fibre of my soul.

If that doesn't sound too dramatic.

And if you think, "Okay, great Jack. Makes perfect sense— you want to fuck this poor little abused student, so you go to the goddamn Bible to find justification. That's great—twist the Bible in any way you want to serve your own lecherous ends. Well, maybe I *was* doing that. But if I was guilty of twisting the Bible, so was St. Bernard. Because there is no doubt in my mind that St. Bernard was telling us that the Song of Songs is about a spiritual connection so great and passionate that it's physical. And to do that, he was conferring validity on the whole physical side of love.

I don't think it's any accident we don't hear much about St. Bernard, except that they named a dog after him. And, of course, I made the old lady in the library find this biography of Malachy that was, of course, written by St. Bernard. And it seemed pretty clear to me that St. Bernard was in love with Malachy. I mean, Malachy was an Irish monk who came to visit St. Bernard in his sunny little monastery in southern France (Clairvaux). And right away, Malachy decides to go back to Ireland and start another Cistercian monastery there. And before you can say "I want to fuck you very badly, brother Malachy," St. Bernard is up there visiting Malachy in Ireland. And then Malachy gets sick and dies in St. Bernard's arms. And St. Bernard is all concerned about

making him a saint. I have a feeling that no one would have
concerned themselves with Malachy until St. Bernard made a
big deal out of it. (He seemed like a pretty neat monk, but no
one was really thinking much about little monasteries in Ireland
at the time.) I mean, St. Bernard is about as knowledgeable and
concerned about the Irish as he is about screwing women. He
calls the Irish "heathens" with "barbaric practices." (I guess
considering the recent "troubles," it's not too far from the truth.
Sorry. I don't mean to offend you if you're Irish.) It's one of
the reasons this biography of Malachy is not too popular—it
trashes the Irish. All St. Bernard is really concerned about in this
biography is Malachy. And every time Malachy comes in to the
room he uses all this the-sun-is-shining-again imagery.

We know what that's about.

So just because St. Bernard probably fucked Malachy, does
that mean I get to do the same thing to Theodore?

No, not just that. I mean, I will admit that since Matthew
wouldn't talk to me anymore I craved advice. And he had given
me this historical religious clue into his ideas about teaching
and learning. So it was a complete philosophical trail that I
could follow. And it was a way of keeping in contact with
Matthew. Even though it's true that I was coming to conclusions that would alarm him. But I just thought, well, he must
have gone down this road once. Even if he rejected it. So in a
weird way, I felt all this stuff with Theodore was part of my
learning process.

I really thought it out. Once I got all these signs from the
Bible, I still tried to figure out if fucking Theodore would be
the best way for him to learn. I even thought about a new gay
theory called "mentoring."

Now, according to this "mentoring" theory, young gay men need
role models. They need people to look up to. The theory is that
young gay men don't know how to lead good and productive lives

because they don't grow up in "gay families." So the whole mentoring project suggests that older gay men should have friendships with younger gay men and try and help them. You know, go out to movies, football games, I guess even drag shows, I don't know, and bond. (If this sounds to you like the whole "Big Brother" concept, you're not that far off. They're very similar.) It's like treating gay kids a bit like homeless under-privileged boys who need older guys to hang out with.

Now when I first heard this concept I hated it with every fibre of my being.

My reaction was pretty visceral.

You see, if there's one thing missing from the whole "mentoring" process, it would be—what? You're right. Sex. No mention of sex at all. In fact, if you're an older gay guy mentoring a kid (meaning teenager), you're not supposed to have sex with him. Now, it seems to me that there is already quite a big "mentoring" thing going on in the gay community, and that would be—what? Yeah. Boy hookers and their clients. I mean, just hang out downtown in the city at night, and you see all the boys lined up on the streets to get paid by the old guys for blow jobs in cars and stuff.

And I know lots of kids who do this or have done this, and I know lots of older guys who buy them.

Now I'm not trying to romanticize prostitution and say it's always wonderful and beautiful. Because it isn't. I'm sure some of these boys would rather not be hooking. And I'm sure it institutionalizes a very personal thing (sex) for them. And for some I think that's difficult.

But after observing these old guys and their tricks at very close quarters for years, I would say two things.

First, a lot of these hookers are really gay and looking for a sex-daddy "mentor." And the only way they can get a sex-daddy, feeling ashamed about their homosexuality, is to make it part of a business deal. In other words, I think some of these guys like sucking old guy's dicks. Or having their dicks sucked by old guys. But the only way to do it in our society is to make it part of a business deal. Or people think you're nuts.

Also, a lot of these hooker-client things are actually relationships. They actually love each other and have long-term affairs. I mean, some clients hire the same hookers all the time. And they talk to them and do lotsa fun things with them besides sex. So there's definitely a mentor thing going on. The older guy has money and worldly experience and the younger guy has beauty, and they trade. And I don't think it's always a bad deal.

If you're going to talk about mentoring, then you shouldn't ignore the mentoring that's already going on in prostitution.

Well, this kind of talk makes all those "gay mentoring" types hit the roof. It's a real mom-and-apple-pie issue. They think it denigrates the whole processs of mentoring by mentioning prostitution in the same breath. Gay mentoring types see prostitution as non-consensual sex, in which the younger guy is victimized. And thinking of these old guys who pick up whores and become their mentors disgusts the gay mentor advocates, totally.

I guess what I think is that sex shouldn't be left out of gay mentoring: to leave it out is to be sexophobic. And you might say, well, what about if a kid wants help and no sex? Well, I would say fine. I mean the relationship is about help, isn't it? But if sex happens, well, why stop it? And you might say, if sex is allowed to enter into the mentoring relationship, then the older, lecherous teacher might seduce the innocent boy against his will. Yeah, right. Only if you believe that teenage boys are sexless and have no will of their own.

And more than that, it's about how much teachers reveal about themselves. The more a teacher reveals, the more profoundly a teacher can teach. The more time I spent teaching, the more important this seemed. I kept thinking about my old therapist who was into boys and didn't tell me. I needed that information. It was denied. All because the "teacher" (the power figure) is not supposed to reveal personal stuff.

And sex is the ultimate revelation. It's about nakedness. It's about being vulnerable and weak and real. All my thinking about the subject made me believe the best way I could teach Theodore was to consent to having sex with him. You probably don't agree. But maybe you don't know what it's like being a gay man. Or maybe you're gay and you don't want to admit this kind of stuff to yourself. Well think about this: when I first came out it was really hard for me because nobody told me how it all worked. And being gay is really complicated. There are bathhouses and open relationships, for example, that I didn't know anything about at first. In fact, when I first came out, it took me a whole year to get laid. And it wasn't because I was ugly. It's because lots of guys didn't want to sleep with me due to my somewhat effeminate nature. (Sometimes I talk with my hands.) At the time, though, I just figured if I was gay, all the other gay guys would love me because I was such a queen. And do you know why it took me so long to learn these important details of gay life? Because all my early friendships were with older men. But they were the wrong kind of mentors—sexless old queens who never gave me any important advice. Hey, they were far too busy trying to show how respectable they were. I was this young gay guy and I just wanted someone to get down and dirty with me and deal with questions such as:

"How can you have an open relationship?"

"What do you do if you're horny all the time?"

"Why do I fall in love with every guy I have sex with?"

Important questions like that. I'll tell you who won't give you real answers to those questions. Some sexless little gay "mentor" who talks pompously about his lover, and their dogs, and their trips to a gay church, and how they're thinking of adopting a child, and commitment ceremonies, and…pardon me while I puke! Oh, the hypocrisy! You can learn a lot about hypocrisy and lying from an uptight little gay mentor. You basically learn that's what the world is about. And you learn not to reveal yourself or be vulnerable about your flaws. A mentor who never gets down, never gets vulnerable, is the very worst thing. I mean, this is about the entire power structure here. Okay, think about it. What if you weren't allowed to teach anybody unless you fucked them, or better yet, got fucked by them? (As you can see, I think it's important to switch the tables here, and make sure you understand that the power-figure guy is not just getting his rocks off. There's got to be an exchange. There's got to be real need and maybe love. The teacher has got to get down on his or her knees to worship the student.) That would make teaching a real proposition. This is pretty much about toppling the power structure, as far as I can see. "Show me your dick, mister, then lick my twat, then we might see some real gay mentoring!"

I don't know. I guess there are some of you out there who — from this point on—will just think I'm a horny old guy trying to fuck some young butt by using every rationalization in the book. Others might understand my arguments. But hey, even if you think I'm a sex fiend, that's okay, because I think sex is a good thing. You can learn a lot from it. A lot more than from books. As old St. Bernard would say, "It is better to love than to study." And you know what kind of love he means. The "human" kind.

In fact, I would go so far as to say the best way to learn from someone is to have sex with them.

There, I said it.

It doesn't mean you always have to have sex with everyone, dummy, in order to learn.

But if someone turns you on, what a great way! What a revolutionary way!

What an honest way.

At this point in my mental contortions I kinda threw all reasoning out the window. I became a missionary, an evangelist of teaching and sex.

So that's where I was when I decided to invite Theodore over to my house.

Which was a very big deal.

I had no one to ask about this. I was very alone (no gay "mentor"). I wasn't quite as close friends with Lyle anymore. I was beginning to suspect that Lyle was falling in love with me. Fags have to watch out for that with their male "girlfriends." I felt bad about losing his friendship. But I thought it best to cool things off for a bit.

And I certainly wasn't going to ask Pat, my only colleague and friend in the department. And Montgomery was off somewhere with a new boyfriend who was even more "much man" than the last one.

It meant it was my decision alone.

So when Theodore rang my bell I took full responsibility. And what a responsibility it was.

I'll never forget the first time he walked into my apartment. It was very dramatic. And it was obvious that, for Theodore, just being given free reign of my place was a big deal. I never really understood why. After all, he supposedly lived with his mother in a huge house in Bunionville. My apartment was a little hole in the wall in the gay village in the city. Why would he be so impressed by it?

But right away, I realized he felt very privileged to be let into my apartment. I think it had to do with the fact that, right off, he had fantasies about living there and being cared for. I mean, basically, his mother was taking care of him, right? That's pretty

humiliating when you're twenty. (Theodore was actually a kind
of old first-year student, because he'd gone off into the worlds
of stripping and drugs after high school.) So, I recognized, as
soon as he stepped over the threshold of my little pad, this was
the beginning of a fantasy for him.

He didn't say anything about the apartment, it wasn't that.
But he immediately started putting himself down.

"Oh my God, you want me to go. You don't want me here."

"Theodore, I invited you."

"No, you don't want me here, I'll go."

"Why don't you think I want you here?"

"You didn't hug me."

"Okay. I'll hug you." I did. "There."

Pause. Then: "That was forced. I should go."

"Theodore, please—"

"No, I know what you're thinking. You're thinking I never
should have invited him over here, he's a freak, he's a nutbar, I
regret having him here." He looked around my apartment. "I
should go."

"I want you to stay." I barred the door.

"Are you sure you're not just saying that?"

"No, I'm not. You can stay."

"Are you sure?"

"Yes."

"Thank you."

"I wouldn't have asked you over if I didn't want you here."

"Really?"

"Yes."

"Oh, that's nice. Kiss me?"

"Sure."

And I kissed him right away, which led to something else.

Him blowing me, actually. It became really clear, really quickly,
that Theodore was an expert cocksucker. In fact, a true profes-

sional. It's hard to describe a really good blow job. Let's just say that he knew exactly how eager to be, how much to look like a little boy, how much to slurp and make noise, how much to beg, and how much to hold off. You get the idea.

Theodore told me later that he did a little bit of hooking along with the stripping. This was not a surprise to me, after the blow job.

And, of course, when he was blowing me, he started jerking off. And there, of course, was the big surprise.

Theodore was hung. And I do mean hung.

This was no ordinary dick. This was definitely monster territory. I remember looking down at him as he was sucking me off and noticing this thing and thinking, Jesus that looks big! And it got bigger and bigger and bigger. It was about eleven inches long. One of those unimaginable dicks. And very thick. It was half the size of Theodore. Of course, the dick explained the stripping. Because Theodore had the kind of body that only a boy-crazed daddy like me could love. He was very skinny and had no tits at all. And his stomach was very flat and muscly. (You could see his ribs.) And then this little boy face and eyes, and then suddenly this dick of death.

I tried not to make a big deal about it. I know some guys with big dicks are quite shy about it. A lot of guys with big dicks are afraid you'll love them just because of their big dicks. And I'm very careful not to. My dick is quite normal (a little on the thick side) so that kind of admiration is not a problem for me. But guys with humungous ones, sometimes they don't even want you to see theirs. Because they know you'll go crazy and start wanting to slurp it all up twenty-four hours a day. A lot of the guys with big dicks (guys like Theodore) really like to suck cock, actually. So I tried not to make a big thing about his "big thing."

But Theodore wasn't shy about his dick (though he liked sucking cock more than getting sucked). He'd sort of make it part of his never-ending monologue, his wacky comedy act: "Do you think my dick is big? I guess it is kinda big. I have to haul it around. Sometimes it's bad. Bad dick, don't do that. Oh my God, it's so heavy, oh my God, I can't pick it up, it's not fair, I'm such a little boy, I've got such a big dick, do you think it's big? Do you? I think it's little. Do you? It's little, really. I'm sorry I have such a tiny dick."

The best way to describe Theodore in bed is to say that he was basically a sex-trade worker. A harem girl. He would do anything you asked. Mostly he sucked me and sometimes I fucked him. One night, he sat on my dick while I fucked him and I watched his gigantic dick spurt. That was certainly edifying.

Another night, he did his strip act for me. Boy, could that kid move.

We were totally compatible, sexually. Then I began to realize that maybe Theodore wasn't quite as interested in sex as me. But I didn't let it become a problem for either of us. Basically (I learned), Theodore was interested in being accepted, in being loved. He wanted desperately to be my boyfriend and move in with me. His conversation was a constant comedy act, built around one theme: "Do you love me?" I'm trying to give you a real sense of this here. He wasn't like Jeannie Berlin. That is, well, did you ever see that movie *The Heartbreak Kid*? Where Jeannie Berlin plays Charles Grodin's cloying wife? He dumps her for Cybil Shepherd, which in this movie seems like a good idea. (I actually do think that Cybil Shepherd is a case of unparalleled beauty triumphing over unparalleled vacuousness—only in the movies!) So anyway, Jeannie Berlin (who is the fabulous Elaine May's daughter, by the way, did you know that?) is hysterical. The greatest scene is where she's eating egg salad (it had to be egg salad, the most disgusting food in the world) and she gets it all over her face. It's almost impossible to watch, it makes you sick. And Charles Grodin is like, "Honey...you've got some food on your face, there." "Oh, do I?" she asks. Anyway, she's cloying and disgusting and always whining, saying, "Do you love me?" Well, the amazing thing about Theodore was that he had figured out ten thousand hilarious ways to say "Do you love me?" over and over without sounding like Jeannie Berlin in *The Heartbreak Kid*. And I just found it very entertaining and fun to tell him that I did, I guess, by responding to his humour. One night (because he knew I used to do drag roles in my early acting days) he decided to scrounge in my closet and find all my old drag and dress up. "You'll love me," he said, "you'll really love me in drag." And then he dressed up very badly. And he looked—well, he looked like an angular boy in a dress. Which is always a frightening thing! The most beautiful boys make bad drag queens, of course. Masculine beauty comes with angles. Theodore had a craggy brow and a nose that was a bit prominent. Even his gorgeous mouth seemed in drag, just ridiculously big and pouty. Like some model with an overdose of collagen. I told him that I didn't find drag queens sexually attractive. But it didn't stop him. He put on a Madonna CD and madly started dressing up, saying, "Don't I look fabulous? Aren't I wildly attractive and don't you want to fuck me?" I didn't. He looked grotesque. I told him to take off all the makeup and the clothes. And then I fucked him.

Theodore was so funny. One night we were watching *Melrose Place* and there was some female character, I think it was Stacey. Whatever, she had a real soap opera name, and she was losing her memory and then, I guess, dying. And Theodore started just going bananas. He was clawing at me, clutching pillows, going, "Oh no, Stacey, don't die. Don't die, Stacey. Please, Stacey, don't die." I remember Lyle happened to call me while this was happening. I picked up the phone for some reason in the middle of it all, and said, "I can't talk right now." And I was laughing hysterically. Lyle said, "I've never heard you laugh like that before."

I never had.

And, of course, it wasn't all about sex and giggling. We talked about serious stuff. He'd come in some nights and say, "An hour ago, I almost did coke." And I'd ask him why, and he'd tell me. Sometimes it would be because he had just seen Big Bob, which was very emotional for him. (They still had to split up the furniture they had amassed from the time they lived together.) I really supported Theodore in his efforts to get off drugs. And I figured if we could have a good time together (a really good time) off drugs, then maybe he would stay off.

He wanted me to meet his parole officer. His parole officer was kind of interested in meeting his new boyfriend. I told Theodore we should wait until the course ended.

I was still teaching him acting two days a week, but that wasn't really where the important learning was going on.

The biggest learning was all about how far he could go. How much he could ask, or, ultimately, demand, of me, in terms of material objects and, finally, money. I spent a lot of time drawing boundaries.

Theodore made himself at home in my house. He slept over a lot and we'd take the bus in to Stony Bay together on the days when we had class. (Of course, we split up when we got off the bus and went our separate ways. We didn't walk into class together and then start finishing each other's sentences and calling each other "honey." We weren't that stupid!) But—I don't know if you've ever had a boyfriend or girlfriend like this—it was a pretty poignant situation. You see, whenever Theodore was at my apartment, I knew that he wanted to stay there forever. And eventually the time would come to kick him out. Maybe I had to work on something and I just needed solitude. But I definitely couldn't work with him bouncing around. He would say, "Okay, tell me to go. Just tell me to go. Here. I'm going now. I'm going!" And he'd pick up his coat. (He had this little fall jacket that made him look quite pitiful. Gee, I couldn't believe that a kid from a family with money would have a jacket like that.) And then before he left, he'd always manage to ask, "Can I come back in a couple of hours?" I'd wrestle with it. Sometimes I'd say, "No." Sometimes, "Yes." And when I said "Yes" I never regretted it. We always found something to do together. Looking back on it, I don't know what. I remember that he cut my hair. I shaved him all over once. (That was very sexy.) We watched TV. We chatted and listened to records and had sex. We went to this obscure gay bar together where hookers hang out with their tricks. (I didn't want people to see me with him yet.) Theodore would go off to talk to some of his friends at that bar. Friends from the sex trade industry. But then, in no time, he'd be back dancing and necking with me. We always had a good time. I don't know why, I can't explain it. And to me that's always love.

But there were subtle ways that he was trying to insinuate himself into my life. He left things at my house. Clothing. (I still have his tiny underwear. How did he fit that dick in there?) And just, I guess, because I did a lot of things for him (bought him lots of beer and cigarettes), he brought things for me. He brought me a beautiful, fluffy towel and shampoo. (I know that doesn't sound like much, but I figured he stole it from his mom's. Which means he went on a dangerous mission for me.) And he brought me a dancing beer can.

And what—you might ask—is a dancing beer can? Well, it's exactly that. It's made out of faux metal and it says "BUD" on it. And it has sunglasses, too. And when you put batteries in it and turn the On lever, the beer can dances to music. Yeah, it's quite a unique device. And actually kind of creepy. The way the can dances is very strange. It kinda writhes about in a creepily human way. And, of course, you don't expect a beer can to dance, so it looks odd. I can't tell you the number of times I came home late (and drunk) having forgotten that I left the dancing beer can on. And, lo and behold, I'd turn on the stereo and the can would suddenly start dancing. And totally freak me out.

I still have that can and it still makes me think of Theodore.

But maybe it's time for me to tell you about the dream.

I think I had the dream because I really thought I was helping Theodore. Sure, I was having sex with him, watching him pull on his big dick. But I was also respecting him, and loving him, and not feeding him coke. And I would have met his parole officer. Really. If certain things hadn't happened. I guess in my heart I hoped Theodore was learning someone could respect him and still fuck him. That's what I hoped.

And the dream I had was all about this old movie. It's weird. I don't even know if this old movie exists. I think I saw this movie when I was a kid, but no one ever seems to have heard of it. So maybe it's just a dream. See what you think.

It was all about a boy who has this caterpillar that he teaches to dance. The caterpillar is really quite great and it lives in this little shoebox. And it does a mean tap dance to "Sweet Sue."

I know the whole thing sounds unlikely, and even more unlikely that all this was in a movie. (How would they get the caterpillar to dance, for instance?)

When I was going out with Theodore I dreamed the dream quite regularly. And I always felt really sad for the boy with the dancing caterpillar. But I didn't know why.

The boy was obviously me, and the dancing caterpillar was obviously Theodore.

Even when I think about it now, I get upset.

It probably had to do with the lumps in Theodore's groin. It was about a month into our relationship, and late into the fall term. And it was about this time that Theodore decided to show me the dancing lumps in his groin.

Now, first of all, you have to realize how skinny Theodore was. He was basically a bag of bones with a huge penis. Which

made me think of AIDS, of course. (When I see a skinny fag
with a big dick I have a surefire way to stop myself from thinking
he has AIDS. I just think of Frank Sinatra. Frank Sinatra, as a
kid, apparently, was a bag of bones with a huge dick. This was
even before AIDS existed! Someone once asked Ava Gardner,
his wife, why she was fucking a 110-pound weakling. She said,
"Because 90 pounds of him is dick." I thought that was so
sweet!) You see, Theodore's cheekbones were quite inverted
and his eyes were quite sunken. All of this made his lips seem
more beautiful than ever, of course. So Frank Sinatra or no Frank
Sinatra, I'm sure that when you read this, you're thinking, the kid
had AIDS for sure, you dumb faggot! Well, what do you take
me for? But we fags (most of us, thank God) use safe sex all
the time these days.

Theodore and I did. I always used a condom when I fucked
him. And cocksucking is low-risk. (We didn't use condoms for
cocksucking! Come on, tell me another joke! Can you imagine
sucking a condom? Well, no self-respecting faggot can either.
Even the AIDS committees say it's low-risk now. Saliva kills
the virus. So don't bug me about that. And of course I wasn't
letting Theodore get anywhere near my ass with that fucking
torpedo of his. So there you go.) But, safe as we were, I still
thought it would be right to ask. So I did. "Did you have the
AIDS test?" I asked him. And he said, "I have one every six
months"— every hooker, even a part-time hooker, knows you
have to get tested —"and I've always tested negative." So this
reassured me. He was awfully skinny. I just put it down to the
coke. Coke does make you skinny, after all. And he was missing
part of his nose.

But then he did a little dance with the lumps in his groin.

Yeah, well, Theodore had these lumps in his groin, one on
each side. And he said, "The doctor says they're hernias, aren't
they neat?" And then he'd push in his abdomen, which was

already so fucking flat it was scary, and he'd say, "Look..." And he'd show me these hernias one after another, sticking out, looking very gross. I'd try to laugh: that was the dance with the lumps in his groin.

I tried to think that this was amusing and that the funny lumps probably were hernias. Being a large person, I probably am very ignorant of the weird things skinny people can do with their bodies. (It's true. It's different having layers of fat; all my inner stuff is hidden. But with really skinny people they're practically wearing their spleens on their sleeve.) But even acknowledging that Theodore was awfully skinny, it did scare me a bit (just like the dancing beer can, for some reason) to see Theodore do the groin dance.

And it made me worry about him, and wonder whether he was telling the truth. And wonder how much he was trying to scare me. Or, more likely, how much he needed love if he had to try so hard to scare me in order to get it.

Like the lesion on his nose.

Why did he use the word lesion?

It just seemed that everything—from the put-downs, to the gifts, to the person either showing off his infirmity or pretending to have infirmities—was about looking for love. All of it.

Anyway, all of this negotiating around space, and giving each other things, and worrying about Theodore's need for love, came to an ugly head. You see, I got this opportunity to lecture at the Andy Warhol Museum.

It was very weird. Something from an article about me had caught the attention of the Andy Warhol people. So they wanted me to come and talk about sex and acting. It was good that at least some people, somewhere, could actually admit that my political work was really about sex. And yet they didn't seem to mind.

The trip to the Andy Warhol Museum was a big deal for me. And I was very excited about it. I'm a real fan. And I know they show the movie *Blow Job* at the Andy Warhol Museum over and over (a thousand times a day), which really excited me. So I warned the university that I would be going away for the weekend to Pittsburgh. And as the date got closer, I began to think that I might let Theodore stay in my apartment while I was gone.

I knew it would mean a lot to him. That was the main reason why I wanted to do it.

But I also...well, it wasn't so much that I didn't trust Theodore. (I really did, he seemed to be off the coke. Sure he was antsy sometimes. But that could just be youthful hijinks, right?) Anyway, let's leave aside the issue of trust. (I figured he might get drunk and stoned, and jerk off, and have friends over; none of this bothered me.) I simply thought that maybe it was too soon to have this intimacy. This taking-care-of-the-apartment intimacy.

Anyway, as you can see, I was all mixed up about it. So in the heat of an "après blow job" one night, I told Theodore that he could take care of my apartment while I was in Pittsburgh. Then, of course, a couple of days later, a week before Pittsburgh, I decided it would not be a good idea. Really, it mostly had to do with thinking Theodore might just want to move in with me after he stayed there. I had this feeling that once he was in my apartment that long, I'd never get him out. I didn't know if I was ready for a roommate. He just seemed a little bit too eager.

I know when I tell you this you might think I got it all wrong. You might think Theodore was lying to me. That he did not live with his mother and he was just a poor, lonely street boy in a bad jacket. But I know he did live with his mother. I talked to her. And she answered the phone saying, "Strong residence." That is his last name—Strong. (I know that for sure, because his full name, Theodore Strong, was on my class list.) And Theodore made me talk with his sister once, on the phone. She was a teenager, and she gabbed away. (She told Theodore that I had a sexy phone voice.) So I know that Theodore's family was real. I talked to them. And flirted with his sister.

But I did a very stupid thing over this whole apartment business. I told Theodore that I changed my mind and he could not stay at my apartment while I was gone. Well, this upset him very much. I think he was angry and hurt. He thought I didn't trust him.

I had a nice time in Pittsburgh. But mainly I missed Theodore. And I went and stood in front of Andy Warhol's never-ending *Blow Job*. It just made me think of Theodore.

And then, when I came back from Pittsburgh, the first time I saw him was in my class. Afterwards, he came up to me and said he wanted to talk. I took him into my office and closed the door. (I figured, what did it matter now?) And then things got very weird.

"Did you have a good time in Pittsburgh?"

"Yes."

"That's good. What were you doing there again?"

"I was at the Andy Warhol Museum, giving a talk."

"Oh yeah, did they like you?"

"They seemed to like me very much."

There was a pause and he stood on a chair next to the window. Then sat on the window ledge. He seemed to always have a need to be high up when he was in my office.

"Remember what I told you once?"

I didn't know what he was talking about. "You told me a lot of things."

I was actually a little terrified that he was really angry and going to break up with me for good.

"I told you—"

He jumped down and sat in my lap and kissed me.

"You break my heart and I break your face."

Oh my God, it was this scary thing he said to me now and

then. It was very good-natured, in a way. But it was also a bit angry. I thought of his dad, who had broken his heart, probably by molesting him. And probably by hitting him, too. And I thought of Big Bob, who had broken his heart, probably without Theodore even knowing it, by feeding him enough coke to almost kill him. And I felt really horrible for not letting him stay in my apartment. He was probably manipulating me at the time, but I didn't know it. I just wanted to help him. I did. And that's how I got into so much trouble.

"Do you like me a little bit?" he asked.

"I like you a lot," I said.

He stared at me.

"You are so hot," he said.

"Thank you," I said.

"I really mean it," he said. "You break my heart, and I break your face."

"I know you mean it," I said. He always frightened me when he said that. But I thought of Jillie, who had said that good sex was always dangerous. Theodore might actually break my face for not letting him stay in my apartment while I was in Pittsburgh. I was sort of hypnotized. There had been no sex in Pittsburgh, mainly because I hadn't wanted any. I had dreamed, not of Theodore's dick (though it had been in my mind), but about the dancing caterpillar (and the dancing beer can, and the groin dance). And there had been lots of crying, and missing him, and writing bad poetry. And now here he was on my lap, kissing me.

"Prove it. Prove you like me a lot."

"Okay."

"Will you do something for me?"

"Anything," I said.

"Fuck me in the toilet."

"What?"

"The toilet down the hall, fuck me there."

"Are you crazy?"

"No. You can sit on the seat like you're taking a dump. I can ride your cock and jerk off. I guarantee I'll come. It'll take me a long time, but I'll come."

Theodore always took a long time to come.

"It's too small," I said. "We could never fit in there."

"What? The bathroom's huge."

"I mean the cubicle."

There was one cubicle in this single-person bathroom. It was a very strange toilet.

I knew saying it was too small was a lame reason. Why wasn't I just saying, "No Theodore, no. Are you out of your mind?"

But I was completely caught up in our love and feeling guilty about Pittsburgh. I thought: it's Friday afternoon, very late (the class went till five-thirty) and the place is like a tomb.

I don't know if you've ever been in a university in the "off" hours. Well, when the place is closed down, it's like you could drop a bomb in there or yell "sit on my face!" and no one would hear.

And I wanted everything to be alright with Theodore and me. I did.

Maybe somewhere inside I knew the whole relationship was impossible, too damn good to be true. So I wanted to ruin it.

Maybe I knew that I loved teaching, so I thought, I'll just wreck my life and fuck it up, because I hate myself.

I don't know.

Or maybe I just loved Theodore a lot.

And the bathroom was very public, but the door could be locked and there was no one around. And so I very, very stupidly said, "Yes."

It was so erotic. I went in to the bathroom first. I jerked off, without locking the door. I got a raging hard-on. I had told Theodore to meet me in there. I figured that if someone found me when I was jacking off, I was at least alone. (I thought,

I could be arrested, like George Michael, for "having a sexual experience by myself" or whatever he was charged with.) Besides, there was no one around. Theodore was going to come in and meet me in a few minutes. If someone had told me this whole thing as a sexual fantasy, I probably would have said that it was too nutty. That I'd be too nervous and I'd never keep my hard-on long enough for anybody to come and sit on it.

But that didn't happen. No sir. I always had a thing for toilets. And this was a very white, institutional one. And it had a mirror, if you can believe it. And you could see yourself in it if you opened the door to the cubicle. So I would be able to see myself fucking Theodore. So there I was, jerking away. And in exactly five minutes Theodore came in and hopped on my cock.

And yes, he remembered to lock the door. (We weren't that stupid!)

And the two of us were off to the races. We must have made a bit of noise in there and it kind of echoed. But we didn't care. It was so great, with all the lights on, to have Theodore sit facing me and jerk off his huge cock. And then he turned around, and I hugged him as I fucked him and I could see both of us in the mirror. He was my boy and I was giving him a great ride. My face looked much too red in the mirror, but his just looked beautiful.

It was at this point, during the high point of our fucking, that we heard the door unlocking. I think we were both in such a state of shock that we didn't disentangle ourselves or shut the door. It all happened so fast, and we were having such a good time.

A woman stood there. I recognized her. She was in her late forties with frowzy red hair. She was the night maintenance lady. I had seen her a couple of times during the mornings and she had admonished me to put my plastic coffee cup in the correct garbage can. (We separated paper from bottles at St. Stephen's.)

She looked at us and screamed.

"You BUGGERS!" she screamed. "You BUGGERS! YOU BUGGERS!" And then she ran out of the room.

I remember at the time thinking it was a very nineteenth-century thing to say. Which reminded me of Matthew and *Alice in Wonderland*, of course.

Well it was the absolutely typical thing for her to say. Why? Because she was kind of a strange lady. She was very lower-class and not too cultured or articulate. I remember once reading a note she had left in that very washroom. (It was frequented by men and women, students and teachers.) On the note was scrawled: "Pls don't leave your bloody tampons. Girlses. Behind the toilet. Have some respect for yourselve and me too."

I always associated the cleaning lady with that ill-spelled and ungrammatical note. So it was absolutely right, in a way, calling us "buggers"—completely accurate under the circumstances, in fact.

Theodore thought it was funny. I guess he didn't really know the gravity of the situation.

Nothing else happened after that. Yeah, I told you about universities. Even the secretaries in the department are champing at the bit to get out by five o'clock. And the professors, well, you can forget them. I think most of them don't even keep office hours at all.

So it was very quiet when she ran off.

And I don't think *I* even fully realized the gravity of the situation at the time. But, of course, neither of us had an orgasm. It was no longer sexy. All I could think about was, will she know who "the buggers" are? Does she know who I am? Will she remember me? Will she tell anyone? Of course she'll tell someone. Maybe she'll just leave a note. An ungrammatical note that says: "Pls don't bugger each other. In the bathroom. You buggerses. Thankyou."

I know that's just too silly. But these are the kind of things that were going on in my mind. Because I guess I just couldn't believe what had happened. And I hoped that maybe it would all blow over. I was wearing sort of trendy clothing that day. (Theodore always tried to get me to dress a little bit more "hip" in class. He said a teacher didn't always have to look like a teacher). Maybe she wouldn't know I was a teacher.

Who was I kidding? She'd scream right out of there and tell her boss, tell everyone. We would be found out.

We got out of there very fast. I suddenly began to get worried. And Theodore was saying, "Don't worry." And then he'd say, "Do you really need the money?" He meant, from teaching. And I said, "Yes." Teaching was my job. I don't act anymore, remember? Even if the Andy Warhol Museum wanted me to do a talk, it didn't mean I would ever actually make any money. I wasn't really famous for Chrissakes.

No, I needed the fucking job and I enjoyed my students, I really did. And now the whole thing was fucked up because of Theodore. It was completely his idea.

When he ran out of the building it was raining outside, which just seemed to make everything worse. And it was a cold November rain. Theodore started jumping around and making splashes in the puddles (just like Gene Kelly), fully enjoying getting wet. I started yelling at him.

"Do you have any idea what just happened? I just lost my job. I just lost my fucking job because of you."

"Maybe you didn't."

And then—maybe it was all the pressure of him wanting to move in with me, wanting to borrow things from me, or maybe it was the crazy differences between our lives—I just lost it and I started yelling at him. I know I wasn't thinking at all of how sensitive Theodore was, or of the consequences of my actions.

"Fuck off, Theodore, just fuck off. If you want to ruin your own life, fine, but don't drag me down into it. Just fuck off!"

And I stared at him.

Lucky it was raining and late on a Friday afternoon and no one saw us.

Not that it mattered.

But after I yelled, the whole relationhip just seemed horrible and stupid and sad. Theodore stared at me, looking like a drowned cat with an enormous penis. I started to get very depressed. It was always the same, it was always going to be the same. (When you're getting rained on, it's really easy to pity yourself, and I did.) What was this craziness? What was I doing with Theodore? I mean, when you get down to it, what do I have in common with him? What did I want but his big dick? I'm fucking crazy. I'm a fucking old lecher and instead of controlling myself, I used this job to sleep with some stupid whore.

The wetter I got, the more I realized that it wasn't Theodore's fault at all. It was completely my fault for saying "Yes" to him, for saying "Yes" in my office. I could have had a friendship with him. I could have acted like the Dapper Dean. I could have been aloof and helpful. And every time Theodore seemed too needy or slutty I could have ignored it. I could have maybe sent him off for some sort of school "counselling."

I felt very sorry for him for having met me.

Why was it whenever I started to get involved with something positive, I sabotaged it? I had to yell at the old ladies in the Jewish Theatre because they hated homosexuals, didn't I? Then I go and have an affair with the most beautiful, perfect man in the universe, only to dump him because he's not a boy with a flat tummy and a perfect ass. And then I don't even have the intelligence or tact to continue the relationship and lie and cheat on him. That's what most fags do all the time. I could be the "Assistant Dapper Dean" by now if I had just sucked up to Matthew and acquiesced and been polite to the old academic farts at parties.

Yes, I could even have fucked Theodore. I could have fucked him on the sly and not told Matthew. I could have lied. I could have had a perfectly good life if I hadn't been so bloody honest and gullible and fallen in love with a twenty-year-old student. I am so stupid and wimpy. How could I be such a wimp? How could I let some twenty-year-old ex-stripper convince me to live out his fantasies in a university toilet? Was I nuts?

Theodore stared at me and then things got really nasty. He yelled at me. "You make me feel like shit," he said. "You make me feel cheap. You always make me feel cheap, you know that?"

I wanted to point out to him that it was his idea to have sex in the toilet, but it would have been too heartless.

So, he ran off and I should have followed him. After what I'd done to him? I made him feel cheap. Just like Big Bob probably, just like everyone who hired him probably. Just like all the dirty old men who stuffed money down his pants. What had I taught him, what had he taught me? Who was I fooling? Nobody. I was just an old lecher. Just like those guys in that movie *Chickenhawk*. And I was plenty wet, too. I had hurt Theodore terribly. I wanted to run after him. But I didn't.

It was a horrible day. Because of my fuck with Theodore I missed my usual bus. That meant I had to wait for one that wouldn't arrive for another hour and a half. I expected the crazy night maintenance lady to come after me at any moment, with the police, yelling, "Arrest the bugger!" Of course, I hoped Theodore would turn up and throw himself into my arms for one of those fabulous kisses. And we could start again. But the night maintenance lady didn't turn up. And Theodore didn't turn up. And then I started to get very anxious about Theodore.

A kid like him would have a hard time dealing with someone like me yelling "fuck off!" to him in the rain. Theodore had a lot of respect and even love for me. Maybe he would throw

himself in a river or something. Or go back on the coke—
which is like the same thing. Or was I just a wrong turn, or
even a "semi-right" turn, in his incredibly fucked-up little life?
Would he just bounce back?

God, I've been loving young men for what seems like hundreds of years. But it seems I still don't understand them.

When I got back to my apartment, the anxious feelings got worse.
It seemed like there were thousands of things in it that were
Theodore's. The drawers seemed to be filled with his underwear,
for instance. And of course I had mistakenly left the dancing
beer can on. I walked into my apartment and put on the stereo,
trying to cheer myself up, and the dancing beer can scared the
life out of me. And then there was the expensive shampoo he
gave me, sitting beside the bathtub. And there was change and
pennies and an old bracelet that he had left. And the bed was
rumpled. And something told me that I would never see
Theodore again.

Not in the same way. In that way we had been.

And it's true. After that incident, Theodore did one of the
biggest disappearing acts I have ever seen. He never turned up at
St. Stephen's again. He never even withdrew from the course.
He just never came back. It's horrible when you realize you loved
someone, and you said something to them that completely fucked
them up. And you ended everything, and you didn't intend to.
It was as if, with Theodore's disappearance, I suddenly realized
he was an incredibly tender and fragile human being. And I had
gone and stomped all over him.

That's my fantasy, anyway.

I don't really know what happened to Theodore. I mean, the
amazing thing is that someone told me later that he was working in this coffee shop. A coffee shop just on the edge of the
ghetto. It was right underneath the People With Aids Foundation and the local AIDS information place, and it had a big

disabled ramp going up to it and everything. Someone told me he worked there and he had dyed his thin, patchy hair blond. And I thought, why would he be working there, at this sort of AIDS coffee shop? Because he has AIDS? Once, I went to the coffee shop and hung out there for a whole day. I expected him to come in on the night shift. He never did. I asked if he worked there and they said that someone named "Todd" had worked there, but not anymore. I never saw him again. And what's amazing is that we both hung out quite a lot in the gay ghetto. I know we both did that. But we never saw each other. Ever. How did he manage to get out of my way? It scared me that someone could just disappear like that.

And I had my dream about the dancing caterpillar again, and it made me sadder than ever. And I realized why: in my dream (or in the movie it was based on, or whatever it was), the boy had to stop performing with his dancing caterpillar.

A caterpillar turns into a butterfly, of course.

And that's what happens to anyone who loves the young. Before you know it, before you can even stop loving them, they metamorphose into something else. And I thought of all the things I should have said to Theodore. Like, I should have said (this was something I practised in my head over and over, long after he disappeared), "Theodore, the best way I can help you is by not helping at all." Because that was the truth. But then I guess I said it to him, already, in a way, by not lending him my apartment. But would he understand that not lending him my apartment was actually a gesture of love? Of trying to teach him?

As I said, I wasn't so sure that I had taught Theodore anything. My self-esteem was very low. I didn't know what I had become. I had forgotten who I had been before St. Stephen's. I couldn't put any more enthusiasm into my classes because I knew I was going to be fired. I actually thought Matthew would just send me a note in the mail. It was weird, continuing to teach and knowing it was over. But not that weird, because people there had never really been friendly to me anyway. And I began to think that this was probably my fate—to be an outsider forever. And being the strange gay teacher who used to fuck Matthew was probably just as outlandish to the other faculty members as being the strange gay teacher who just fucked some kid in the toilet. If they knew. If they all knew. I didn't know what to think…I was in limbo. So when the summons came—the summons to go and see Matthew—I knew exactly what it was about. And I thought, okay. Humiliation time. Might as well get it over with.

It was one of those cold December days when it's not snowing heavily, but there are some snowflakes whirling around. And it seems bitterly cold just because it's the first day that's cold at all. I thought, I haven't even been teaching at St. Stephen's for a year.

His very gorgeous and efficient secretary told me to go into his office and I went in. I had been there before.

Matthew had hidden his office in a small room at the very top of the college in a very old building. To some, it seemed unpretentious. I realized that even though his office was technically unpretentious, it was probably one of the most interesting rooms in the university. That's the kind of sneaky thing Matthew could get away with—having the most beautiful, fascinating office in the university and still somehow fooling everyone into thinking he was just a humble, self-denying monk and this was his little cell.

It was tiny, but there was an enormous, curved window in the cupola that looked down on the main walkway of St. Stephen's. The room seemed nestled in the trees. It was like a little boy's tree house. I thought of how far we were from being little boys, and how that was somehow really the whole problem.

Matthew was standing in front of the cupola window, looking out, his hands behind his back. It was a thoughtful pose. I

would like to think it was spontaneous, but knowing him I'd
have to say it was completely planned. He turned around, and
he looked perfect. And he was almost smiling. Yes, believe it or
not, he was. But it was not a cordial, loving smile. Not a real
smile. It was instead an extremely distant smile, like the kind of
smile you give visiting dignitaries. It was a duty smile. It was a
smile that said, "Despite all the nastiness, despite your incredible
stupidity, for instance, I can still be gracious." And he was. And
I thought of the time I went to hug my grandmother when she
was mad at me for not fighting in the war. She had simply moved
her hands away. And I had hugged the air.

He was very gracious, and handsome, and absolutely brim-
ming with anger. It was interesting to watch, actually. Here was
someone really deft at handling people now handling a really
horrible mess. That's what I was: *A Really Horrible Mess.*

"Sit down," he said.

I sat down.

He cleared his throat, "This is not a pleasant situation, is it?"

I found myself speaking with a voice filled with anger. An
anger I didn't even know I possessed.

"You tell me," I said.

It was a mistake to even show the slightest anger. It gave
Matthew a chance to show how well he could rise above it.

"Ah." He opened a file. "So, Jack, it seems I was wrong. You're
just not a St. Stephen's sort of person."

"And what kind of person would that be?" I asked, gazing at
him levelly. I really was acting like an idiot.

"I don't think I need to tell you. So—"

"So you're firing me. I know that. But I want to know what
kind of person I am not." Really, I was shaking all over. It was
like someone else was talking, not me.

"All right." He stood up, with my file in his hand, and walked
over to the window. He looked like the perfect, aging, but still

sexy, don. He even managed to have a lock of hair fall casually over his face and brush it away. He spoke very quickly and unemotionally. I think the whole sex part of my "situation" embarassed him. Here we were, talking about sex in broad daylight. He didn't have a glass of wine in his hand. How could he cope? "The fact that you were caught, by the cleaning staff, having sex with one of the students in a washroom, is not the kind of behaviour that, quite obviously, we expect from teachers at this university. In fact, I think you should be very glad that we've decided not to bring charges against you. I understand the student in question is withdrawing from the college. I think this is best for all concerned and—"

I leaned over his desk and I put my hand on the table.

"I only did what you told me."

"What?" He turned around. All stunned, graceful confusion. Perfect. "What do you mean?"

"I'm only following your directions."

"I still don't understand what you're talking about."

"One night, you told me that I was a monk, and this was a monastery, and there were deprivations and denial. And so I thought you just meant not to fuck the students. But you refused to talk to me after that night. That night in the mansion when you came begging for me, begging me to come back—"

Oh, he didn't like me talking about that. He was looking a bit pale.

"I still don't understand—"

"Of course you wouldn't understand. You were drunk. Of course you don't remember anything. But I found out that you're the one who named this place St. Stephen's. And that you named it after St. Stephen Harding. The saint with the same last name as you."

"Ah." He sat down. He seemed genuinely interested. A good gambit on his part, I thought. Very cagey.

"And I did a little research in the Religious Studies library. And I know all about St. Bernard—that's me, John Bernard Spratt— appearing at the monastery. That's St. Stephen's, of course. And bringing with him all his brothers. I assume that's all the fags that you figured would follow me here. Because that's all you ever think about, isn't it? St. Stephen's. Everything is always about St. Stephen's. Maybe that's why you're so unashamed of being calculating, is it? Because it's all for St. Stephen's. Every lie, every manipulation. All for a good cause. Well, I read what St. Bernard wrote. You know who I'm talking about, the monk who had the affair with Malachy. And I read the sermons on the Song of Songs. And it says, and let me quote, 'Let him kiss me with the kiss of his mouth.' And he talks about it being a carnal kiss, a carnal kiss that one man gives another. And I didn't have anyone to talk to about this. So I assumed. Actually, I knew. It was you telling me that the carnal was holy and that teaching was sex and that sex was teaching. And that it was all right for me to fuck one of the students. I did it because you told me to, Matthew. I did it because it's what you taught me. Because I'm your student. And that's the learning that I brought with me to the world."

I was almost crying.

There was a pause. I thought I had been remarkably eloquent. I was completely surprised at my own emotion, though. I wanted to prove something to him. Clearly, I still loved the old guy in some way. And I meant what I said.

Matthew laughed. But it wasn't in that strange, uncontrolled laugh he had. It was very quick and low and brutal.

"Have you gone quite insane?"

We were sounding like an old British movie now. And I almost came back with a Noel Cowardish rejoinder like, "Why, I'm saner than I've ever been before!" But I just said, "No, I'm not. But I think one of us is insane, I can tell you that."

He chuckled again. It was horrible. He looked at me as if he had just, that moment, discovered something about me.

"You're not terrifically intelligent, are you?"

I didn't know what to say to that. I didn't expect him to say that at all.

He answered his own rhetorical question. "No, I'm afraid you're not. I overestimated you. I thought you were St. Stephen's material. But the fact of the matter is, you're not too smart. It's a shame really, because you express yourself well, when you want to. But you so rarely take the time to actually think before you commit yourself to an idea."

He had caught me completely off guard with his vicious, not-so-veiled attack. But fortunately, I have complete confidence in one thing. If only one thing alone: my intelligence.

"I'm very intelligent," I said.

"I see, but speaking of St. Bernard of *Clairvaux*"—he pronounced the place name with an exaggerated French accent, as if to prove I didn't even know the guy's proper name—"did you actually read all of the *Sermons*? Or did you just read *On the Kiss*?"

"I read *On the Kiss*," I stammered, "and other—"

"But you didn't bother to read the entire text, did you? That's the problem, really. You're not a scholar. You're not a thorough thinker. You're a secondary source man. Listen, you can't just read one little sermon from *On the Kiss* and imagine you've got the gist of St. Bernard. You're probably not at all interested, but it's actually a Catholic interpretation of a passage from the Bible."

"I'm aware of that—"

"But you have obviously not read the whole text. And if you ever do, you will realize that, for instance, St. Bernard actually symbolically names each of a woman's breasts. 'One breast is hope,' Bernard said. 'And the other is charity.'" He leaned back in his chair. "Think about it for a minute. Use your brain thoroughly for once. One breast is hope, the other charity. This is a twelfth-century religious manuscript. It is about the nature of communications from God. It is not there to be utilized as a justification for your silly debauches. This all turned out badly, I expect, because I thought you were intelligent, really I did. But you're not."

This was too much. I was suddenly back in graduate school again, and I was being derided for using secondary sources, for having an undergraduate response. Damn it, my response was my response, and I was going to stand up for it.

"And you call yourself a teacher?" Oh, this was good. I was warming to my theme. "You call this a school?"

"I'm afraid I do, yes."

"And what do you teach? You teach lies and hypocrisy. You teach adolescents how to grow up and become boring adults. In hiding yourself from them, you perpetuate an established order which ensures that they will never really grow or question anything. This is not a school, it's a fucking holding tank for boring upper-class kids while they get inculcated with the cynicism and fatuosity of their rich parents."

He leaned back in his chair and glanced out the window.

"There is no such word as fatuosity, Jack."

"I just made it up for you. And I just made one up for me." I stood up. "I am Doctor Mellifluus, that's what I crown myself. The Honey-sweet Doctor, just like St. Bernard. And maybe the difference between you and me is that books are alive for me—they actually mean something, they affect my life, they are dangerous—unlike for you and this dusty old place where ideas are just something to be put on a shelf somewhere and sneered at, or collected, and analyzed! I know what learning is because it takes time, and it takes my heart, and it takes my fucking gut to learn anything! This place isn't about learning! Fuck you!"

"Ah, yes, that was very articulate."

"Fuck you and your fucking articulateness!"

And with that I knocked a couple of things off his desk and marched out of the room. And I thought, great, Jack, there you go. Now you've managed to say "fuck you" to the two men you loved the most at this goddamn place.

And maybe that's good, I thought. Maybe it's a good thing.

I pulled my coat up to the blustery cold as I stood at the door of St. Stephen's. I looked out across the main passageway of the campus. I thought about teaching and fucking and fucking and teaching. And I thought: well, great. Maybe I'm going to be a different kind of teacher. And maybe the stuff I have to teach doesn't belong in this place. And never will. That's okay, too.

And then I saw my friend Montgomery, the Divinity student, huddling by a tree with two other black guys. They were clustered together, chatting about something. And these two Black guys were all dressed up like Muslims, and it occured to me they might be fundamentalists. This really got me worried. Gee whiz, Montgomery was pretty gay. But he was also religious. What would happen if he got all involved with one of those woman-hating, fag-hating fundamentalists?

I could catch a later bus back to the city.

For the moment, I made my way across the windy campus, oblivious to the cold. I wanted to talk with Montgomery, that's all. Talk for a while. Then, sure, maybe fuck a little bit if we wanted. Then talk again. I just wanted to have an exchange. Of ideas. And if the talk, or the exchange, or whatever, turned out to be a little bit about God, that would be okay, too. It certainly wouldn't be a bad thing if God somehow got involved with it.

I just wanted to kiss Montgomery, really.

His lips were so luscious and tasty.

If you know what I mean.